LIKE A CURSE

More Magical Reads by Elle McNicoll

A Kind of Spark

Show Us Who You Are

Like a Charm

LIKE A CURSE

ELLE McNICOLL

RANDOM HOUSE NEW YORK

 Published in the United States by Random House Children's Books, a division of Penguin Random House LLC, New York. Originally published in paperback by Knights Of, London, in 2023.

Random House and the colophon are registered trademarks of Penguin Random House LLC.

Visit us on the Web! rhcbooks.com

Educators and librarians, for a variety of teaching tools, visit us at RHTeachersLibrarians.com

Library of Congress Cataloging-in-Publication Data is available upon request.
ISBN 978-0-593-64952-7 (trade) — ISBN 978-0-593-64953-4 (lib. bdg.) —
ISBN 978-0-593-64954-1 (ebook)

The text of this book is set in 12.5-point Sabon LT Pro.
Interior design by Michelle Crowe
Key illustration by Claudia Balasoiu/stock.adobe.com
Sparkles artwork used under license from Shutterstock.com

Printed in the United States of America
10 9 8 7 6 5 4 3 2 1
First Edition

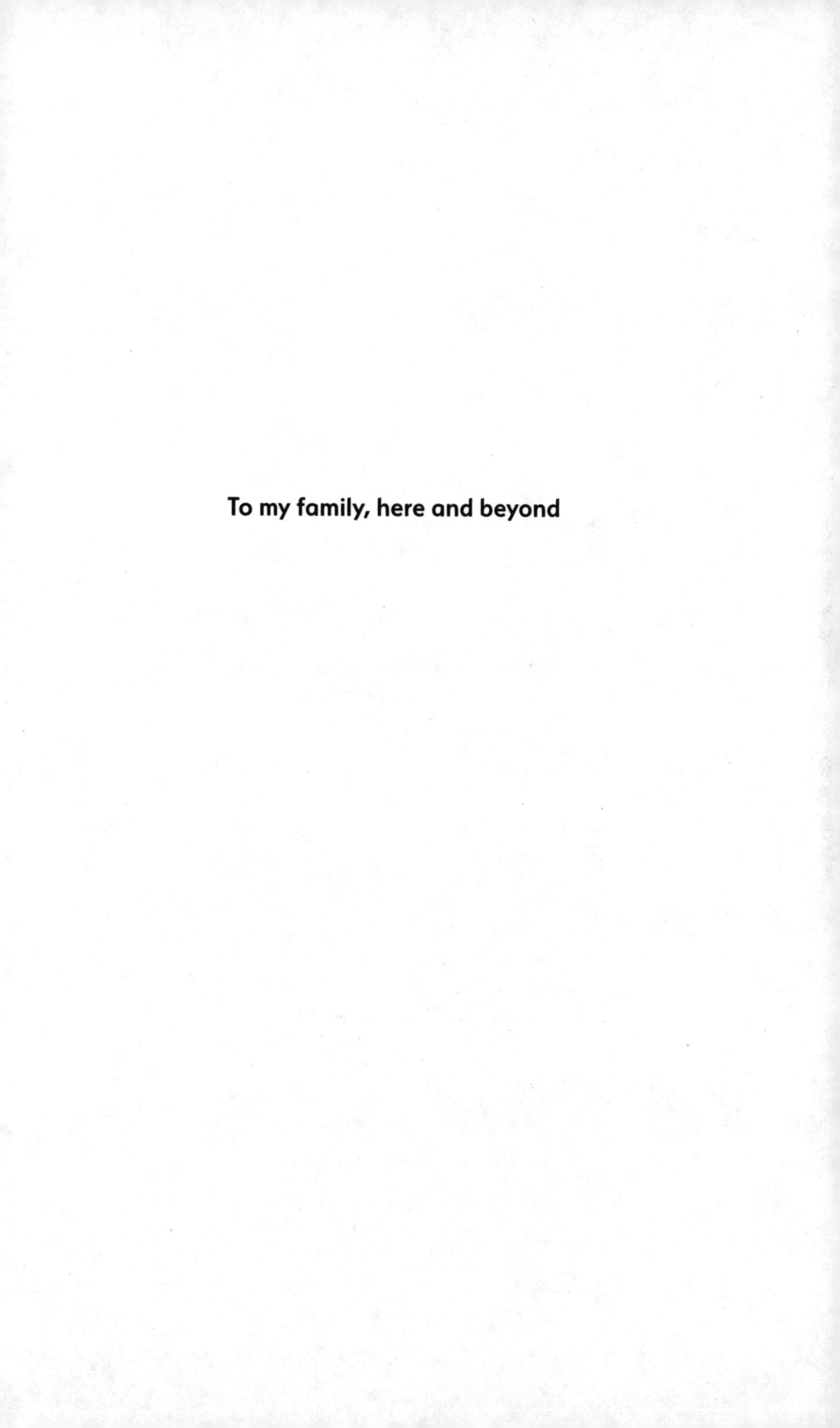

To my family, here and beyond

AUTHOR'S NOTE

The protagonist of this story has been diagnosed with dyspraxia, more formally known as developmental coordination disorder (DCD). It affects motor skills and processing. I was diagnosed at the age of nine. It makes my handwriting messy, but, like Ramya, no one has ever been allowed to tell me what I can or cannot do.

PROLOGUE

EDINBURGH IN DECEMBER

Evil arrived in the city with a beautiful voice and a golden key around her neck.

Saint Giles was the patron saint of Edinburgh, and the cathedral that bore his name stood in the Old Town like a towering elder, disapproving and intimidating. The rain lashed against the ancient stonework: a building that had been there for centuries, longer than any of the people who lived in its city.

With the exception of a few Hidden Folk.

Marley Stewart-Napier was inside. One of his many extracurricular activities at school was singing in the choir, the reason he now waited inside the great cathedral. His choirmates sat all around him, and he could sense that they were as eager as he was to sing. As soon as they sang through all the carols, the concert would be over. They could have a quick glass of orange juice while the parents and visitors drank mulled wine, and then they could all go home. They had wasted an entire day rehearsing, and they were all well and truly sick of the building, no matter how impressive it was.

He was ready to go home.

The cathedral was full of people, every seat occupied by an expectant face. Marley searched and searched but could not find the ones he wanted.

His cousin Ramya was with their aunt and grandmother up in Loch Ness, that he knew. However, his mother and Ramya's parents had promised to be there.

But Marley could not see them.

He did, however, lock eyes on a face he had *not* been expecting. He blinked and then squinted, wondering if he was imagining it. An older boy with blond hair and cold eyes.

"Welcome to this year's highly anticipated Christmas Carol Service," boomed Mitch, their choirmaster, pulling Marley's attention away from the other boy. "We are ready to begin with our first selection and ask that you please turn off your mobile phones."

Parents did just that while others inspected the concert program. Marley and the rest of the choir began to take their positions, standing in accordance to voice range. They were about to receive their first note from the organ, Mitch standing before them all like an overly serious metronome, when everything changed.

Everything.

The enormous, heavy doors at the entrance of the cathedral burst open, the noise and sudden movement causing people to turn with shallow gasps. The candlelight in the large hall quivered and shrank away from the sudden, uninvited arrival of the outside storm.

Marley realized what they were witnessing before anyone else. For standing in the entranceway was someone he had only ever heard stories about. Terrible stories.

She stood with a man who was gaunt and frightening—a man who made no attempt to hide the dark magic that so obviously resided in him. And from the shadows moving behind them, Marley knew more accomplices lay in wait.

When she smiled, Marley could see people in the rows closest to her smiling back, and he knew the room was a barrel of powder merely awaiting a lit match.

"Good evening," she said, her voice causing physical reactions from almost every person in the great hall. "Sorry I'm late."

Portia. Portia had come to Edinburgh. A flame ready to burn everything down.

Marley was about to move when he felt someone grab his arm and haul him behind a pillar.

Freddy Melville. His cousin's siren friend. The boy he had seen sitting in the crowd.

"Are you a part of this?" Marley hissed, feeling indignant and scared all at once.

"No," Freddy murmured, glancing out at the congregation and its newest arrivals. "But I had a suspicion."

"What do we do?"

"We get you out of here. Leanna and Cassandra are waiting outside."

Marley's mother and his aunt. Two of Edinburgh's witches. The former mildly gifted with healing magic and the latter a rather fearsome commander of fire.

Then there was Aunt Opal. The most powerful witch Edinburgh had seen for some time. And his cousin Ramya was now Opal's apprentice. She was the chosen one, Marley thought. He was just the boy who ran around behind her. Ramya could see through Glamour. Ramya could command water. Ramya could fly.

All Marley could do was stand by her side and be impressed by all of it.

There was no other reason for Portia's arrival. She was there for his cousin. His gifted cousin who would grow to be another one of the most powerful witches of Scotland. And therefore was a threat to Portia and other supernatural creatures who wanted to suppress the Hidden Folk.

Marley's eyes narrowed as he peered at the siren boy. He was far more reluctant to trust Freddy than Ramya was.

"We need to sneak out the back," Freddy said, ripping his eyes from Portia to direct Marley toward the exit behind them. Unable to think of any better option, Marley swallowed and started to crawl, careful to remain hidden from Portia, her henchmen, and the rest of the congregation. He felt guilt and worry for all those innocent people fill him up as he dragged himself to the door.

He knew what it was like to be under a siren's spell.

He would not wish it on anyone.

As he reached the heavy wooden door, Marley realized Freddy was not beside him. He glanced back and froze. The other boy stood in the heart of the cathedral, staring down the rival siren with a defiance that made Marley ashamed. He crept out the door and dashed, slipping as his harried feet met the wet stone of the city.

Then he saw them, his mother and aunt, gesturing frantically from his aunt's expensive car. He bolted for them, flying into the backseat with the speed of a bullet.

"Freddy's still inside," he panted, putting his seat belt on without thinking and pressing his nose against the car window.

"He's staying behind, sweets," Leanna said softly.

Marley's head snapped around to stare at the two witches. "What?"

His aunt Cassandra was already driving, causing the car to rip away from the Royal Mile and the noble cathedral that now belonged to a siren. Marley bellowed a cry of despair for the siren friend of his cousin, appalled at the abandonment.

But a plan was in motion.

Inside Saint Giles, Freddy stared back at Portia. Two sirens facing off while the humans watched in fear and confusion.

"Ramya and Opal are gone," he told her flatly. "But they will soon know that you're here."

Portia smiled, and it was clearly not what Freddy had been expecting. It knocked what little triumph he had been feeling clean out of him.

"Fabulous," she said smoothly. "I'm relying on it."

Then she opened her mouth and sang. So rich and compelling was the song that all the humans were helpless.

The golden key around her neck caught the light, flashing showily as the city fell under a siren's spell.

CHAPTER ONE

THE OAK TREE

I can see that the tree has moved. It's a little closer to the house than it was yesterday.

"Ramya? Ramya!"

I know Gran is asking me something. Or telling me something. Yet I cannot stop staring at the tree. Pondering how it could possibly have moved since last night. It's an oak tree, and I noticed it when Mum and Dad first dropped me off here. Mum said it wasn't there when she and her sisters were younger. Even Gran seemed a bit puzzled by it.

"Ramya, stop daydreaming for five seconds and try the spell again."

I'm sitting at the breakfast nook in Gran's large kitchen.

There's an AGA stove and a large fireplace. I

know what I'm supposed to be casting, but I'm not Mum. I'm not so good at fire.

Gran is pretending to be preoccupied with her mortar and pestle, getting the seasoning ready for dinner, but I can tell by the way her shoulders sit that she is concentrating on my task instead.

I'm not allowed to attempt fire by myself, not ever.

I focus on the empty space in the wall where the wood is waiting for a flame.

I concentrate on what Aunt Opal always says. Focus on the doing and not the trying. She always says we don't *try* to do the things that are most important, we just do them. Magic is no different.

But this still feels more like trying than doing.

Gran must sense my growing frustration, because she briskly moves to the window and says, "Were you staring at that oak tree?"

I glare down at my empty palms but take the olive branch. "Yes. It seems like it's getting closer to the house."

"It's probably just growing taller," she counters, but she doesn't sound completely convinced.

It's winter; in Scotland that means the dark creeps in during the afternoon. It's dusk and we are so remote, far from any urban life at all.

That does not include Hidden Folk. They are

scattered all around, and they like to visit Gran's giant house.

Loch Ness is so different from anywhere I've ever been.

While other lochs in Scotland are little blotches on the map, Loch Ness is a long and straight splinter. I expected it to be like a traditional lake, a wide body of water that lets you see the other side. Like the Forth in Edinburgh or Loch Morlich near Aviemore.

But Loch Ness is endless. Slender, but as deep as fresh water can be.

I haven't asked any of the Hidden Folk about the rumors Loch Ness is famous for. I'm a little afraid of what they might say.

I see some coming toward us, carrying a basket. "What are they?" Gran asks carefully.

She can't see through their Glamour, their human disguises, like I can. But their unusual packages, and their uninvited presence, give them away.

"Troll," I say nonchalantly. "One Blue Man. And a Hulder."

They reach the door and knock. This seems to be a regular occurrence at Gran's house, and it made me nervous at first. However, Opal says the house is protected by Old Magic. An ancient spell from an ancestor, making the house untraceable to anyone who wishes its occupants harm. That's the kind of spell I want to learn to cast.

I fling the door open and welcome the Hidden Folk into the foyer. They are friendly and warm and they drop their Glamour for Gran, but we're not who they are here to see.

"Is she here?" asks the troll. "We've brought gifts for the Winter Solstice."

Gran directs them to the large table in the middle of the hall. It's more of a foyer than a hall—I like that her and Grandpa's house resembles the one from Clue. Two doors on the right, leading to the kitchen and dining room. Two on the left for the living room and Grandpa's study.

It's dusty because Gran never lets anyone inside it.

There is a fireplace in the hall, and I try to start a small fire. I concentrate with ten times the might it takes me to bring water. I'm supposed to be keeping these powers a secret, but in this moment, I don't care. I want to be impressive. I want to cast the spell on my own.

I don't understand why fire is so much harder for me.

"Opal is indisposed," Gran says curtly, inspecting the basket of goods these Hidden Folk have brought for the hearth. "Is there a problem?"

Her voice is flinty. She is someone who insists on the house always being warm, and the meals that she prepares always piping hot, but there's a coolness about her at all times. She seems as cold as the water of the loch. Her white hair and pale eyes make me think of a snow queen.

"No problem," the Blue Man says cheerfully. He looks directly at me, and his brow furrows. "Are you a little witch?"

I open my mouth to proudly claim so when Gran cuts across me. "No, she just has the Sight. Only one witch in this house at present."

I glower at her but say nothing. That was the condition of me coming here to learn. My powers were to be kept a family secret.

As if we needed another.

"Well, it's not a problem," the Hulder says, and her voice is nervous. Nervous enough to make Gran glance over at her with a sharpness, a look that demands the facts and none of the dressing. "Not a problem, per se."

"Speak."

Gran has no time for tiptoeing around a topic. She enjoys conversational sledgehammers.

"There's fae in the area," the troll says quietly. The words are enough to freeze the entire house.

The Blue Man and Hulder both wince at the blunt words. I can no longer feel the warmth coming in from the kitchen.

Gran is as still as the water in the loch outside

our front door. It's strange to see her so motionless. She's always busying herself with something. There's always something to check, something to test, something to manage. Now she stands too still. Waiting.

The fire in the hearth suddenly crackles and flares, burning brightly and causing most of us to jump. The Hidden Folk stare behind my head, up at the staircase.

"Who has seen them?"

I turn to gaze up at Aunt Opal. She's wearing a long dressing gown, and her hair is damp. She appears calm and collected, but her green eyes are fixed on the troll. I know what it feels like to be on the other end of her intense gaze.

"You're here," the Hulder says breathlessly. "We heard rumors you came back—"

"Who has seen the fae?" Opal cuts across the fawning with the direct question.

"By the loch," the Blue Man says. "I barter with some Hidden Folk there. One said she saw them."

"What would they be doing all the way up here?" I ask. I speak mostly because I want Opal to look at me, but she does not.

Fae are dark creatures that cannot lie. I met too many for my liking back in Edinburgh. Sinister and malevolent—I was hoping never to run into them again.

"They're searching for something," the Hulder says. The other two Hidden Folk throw her glances that seem to say "Keep quiet." "Well, they are! And we all know what they want to find . . ."

"What?" I ask hungrily.

The Hulder looks over at me, and I can see my own curious expression reflected in her wide eyes.

"A monster!"

"That's enough," Gran says smartly. "Ramya? Ramya, where are you going?"

I move to the front door, ignoring Gran's curt calling of my name. I rush down the stoop toward the stones and the trees and the water. The vast loch stretches out before me like a flowing road. It's as calm as my aunt, but water holds secrets better than anything. I glance around for fae, knowing their Glamour will not conceal them from me.

I see nothing but the stillness of the water.

My cousin Marley once told me it is deeper than you can imagine. Deep as the sea.

"Ramya. Come inside this minute!"

"What do they want to find?" I call back over my shoulder, my eyes scouring the loch, searching for any sign of the unknown. "Why would they come here? What monster?"

My feet are suddenly an inch off the ground. I yelp, wondering if one of the very creatures we were discussing has grabbed me. However, as I slowly float back toward the open front door of Gran's enormous house, I realize who is casting the spell.

Opal is leaning in the doorway, using only one hand to conduct her magic. Gran and the three Hidden Folk watch from the hall of the house, until Opal shuts the door with a pointed click, so that the two of us are alone outdoors. I wriggle against invisible bindings before she drops me unceremoniously on the steps in front of her. I glare up into her face, and she looks coolly down into mine.

"Don't run off around these parts," she finally says, her voice soft and laced with a little menace.

I'm not entirely sure why I do it, but I turn and blast as much magic as I can muster. It becomes a little ball of light, rocketing toward the great loch and breaking like a small firework, high above the wide, murky surface.

I turn triumphantly back to Opal, frowning as I see that her face is blank of any reaction.

"Why not send up a red flare so they can really know where we are?" she finally says.

I grimace. "You said this house is impossible for bad people to find."

"Let's not test that theory, shall we?"

"When do lessons start again?"

"Have you read the books I gave you?"

"No."

"Have you done your schoolwork?"

I grunt and flex my hands. "No."

"Then lessons are not back on."

"Why should any of that matter? Why do I need to do English homework in order to do witchcraft?"

"No one likes an uneducated witch."

"Says the witch who dropped out of school."

Her mildly amused expression darkens and she grabs my wrist, jerking me forward a step. "Exactly."

I should not have said it, but I get riled by her. I can see through Glamour, but not her. Her walls are rarely down.

"I want to try flying again."

I say the words with as much pleasantness and peace as I can manage. I'm trying to behave. I know I don't act the way they want me to all the time, so I need to show them I can be better. If they want me to earn the right to witchery, I'll do it. I'll show them.

"Not yet," she says. I'm about to argue, but she shushes me, her eyes darting about. She moves down the stairs and onto the path. Out of the gate and along the bank of the loch. I listen, trying to pick up on whatever it is she can hear.

A car. A car driving speedily along the road toward the house. The road leading to Drumnadrochit. The road situated between the bank of the loch and the great slabs of land that are steep and tall.

"Tell the Hidden Folk to leave," Opal instructs me, her eyes never leaving the faint headlights that are presently far away but are only growing nearer. "Now."

I move to obey. As I reach the door, I inspect the oak tree once more.

It has, at some point this evening, moved closer again.

CHAPTER TWO

REUNITED

Gran leads the Hidden Folk through the kitchen and out the back door without asking a single question.

I find that quite amazing; if I told my mother to do something, I would be hounded with a thousand follow-up demands, and then I'd be told not to give orders.

No one in the family questions Opal when it comes to the weird or the witchy.

When Gran returns to the hall, I cannot stand it anymore. I run to the front door and fling it open once again.

Three witches and my cousin Marley stand at the gate to the house.

Aunt Leanna. A healer who can make plants and flowers bloom.

Cassandra, my mum. Hard, tough, and capable of setting this entire house ablaze.

Then, Aunt Opal. Who can do anything.

I don't look at them for long; I turn to my cousin. We're the same age, but that is probably all we have in common. Right at this moment, he seems dazed and a little afraid.

Which worries me.

"What's happened?" I fire the words at them.

Leanna and Mum exchange a glance, and there is hidden communication there. It needles me when the three of them have their secret conversations.

"Sirens. Portia."

My gaze jerks to Marley. He was the one who said the words, clearly going against the wishes of his mum and mine.

"She's here?" I ask. "In Scotland?"

"In Edinburgh," Leanna says quietly. "We've been planning—I mean, we always said if she came, we would have to leave."

"But we're just regrouping here, right?" I say, stepping back to let the four of them enter. "We're going back to fight!"

All four adults turn to stare at me. Leanna is worried, Gran and Mum look as if they are about to reprimand me, and Opal's face, as ever, is unreadable. "I don't know, Ramya," Marley says. "She's scary. Different."

"I know, I've met her," I snap. I feel instantly guilty when he flinches at my tone.

But I have met her.

I met her so many years ago. A party in our house when I was small. She could put all the adults in the room under some strange sort of spell with her voice, even Mum and Dad.

But not me. I saw through her. Even if I couldn't quite say what I was seeing.

★

WE'RE ALL SITTING AROUND THE TABLE. Marley is behaving himself and eating his stew. I can barely touch mine.

"We *are* going to stop her, right?"

I ask the question loudly enough to startle Aunt Leanna out of a trance. Mum exhales and glances at me. "Don't be silly."

"What do you mean?" I stare at all of them; none of them will look back. "Who knows what she's going to do to—"

"There's no point being hysterical or jumping to imaginary conclusions," Mum interrupts me. "Best to just lay low."

Gran gets up to leave the kitchen, but I'm too

stunned at Mum's words to take much notice. "Lay low? Because that worked so well last time. Letting Ren waltz in and almost kill—"

"Enough."

I stare at Opal, who was the one who spoke the word, softly but with great intention. "It's true, though," I say.

"You don't have to speak every opinion you have, Ramya. Not everything is black and white."

None of us have ever really spoken about what happened on Inchkeith island. Aunt Leanna's partner, and Marley's would-be stepfather, was secretly a siren. A magical creature that appeared, sounded, and behaved like any other human. Except a siren's voice holds extreme power. They are deeply persuasive and influential, and if they are strong enough, they can make people do things that they do not want to do.

Ren abducted Marley and lured me to the island, and he probably would have killed me if Aunt Opal hadn't arrived. She used her witchery to turn Ren to stone.

Now no one speaks of it. Even though it changed everything.

That was the night I discovered the true nature of my own magic. It was so much more than being able to see through Glamour. It was an affinity with water. The ability to move things without touching them.

Flying.

Opal says I'm not allowed to even attempt flying without her present. The whole thing is frustrating. I'm special. I'm different. I should be allowed to celebrate and bask in that glow, but the whole family wants me to be quiet and cautious.

And hidden. Just like other magical creatures.

I don't want to be hidden.

The phone in the kitchen rings shrilly, causing the adults to jump and start in their chairs. I get up and grab the old receiver and let out a sigh.

"Hello?" I say grumpily.

"Hey, kid!"

I smile, despite the bad mood I'm determined to be in. "Hey, Dad. How's London?"

"Oh, it's . . . it's fine. Listen, bub, your mum isn't answering the landline at home, I was wondering—"

"Yeah, she's here. So is Aunt Leanna."

I hear him exhale in relief while Mum gets to her feet and holds out her hand for the phone. I clutch it more tightly and shake my head at her. "And—"

"Can you put Mum on, Ramya? I need to tell her—"

"About Portia? Yeah, we know. She's in Edinburgh."

I can hear Dad's shocked silence on the other end of the line, and Mum starts clicking her fingers at me, which she knows I find enraging.

"Dad, they're saying we all have to lay low. It's not fair, I want—"

The phone suddenly flies out of my fingers, and I spin around to watch it soar into Mum's hands. I still have to get used to the fact that she is also a witch. She kept it from me for so long.

Her affinity is fire. The opposite of mine.

"Hi," she says stiffly into the receiver, fixing me with a cold glance. "She's fine, just overexcited."

Aunt Leanna pulls me into her lap and gives me a squeeze. I don't know if it's her particular brand of witchcraft, but some of the anger and tension releases out of me. She jiggles me until I roll my eyes and smile slightly. I peer over at Marley, and my smile slips as I see he is staring into space, completely expressionless.

"Marley?"

He glances at me. "Yeah?"

"Did you . . . did you see her?"

He doesn't answer because he does not have to.

His face tells it all. I don't even need him to answer or explain.

I remember what it is that he's feeling. It was years ago when I saw her for the first and only time. I still remember it.

Mum finishes her conversation with Dad and passes the phone back to me. I get up from Leanna's knee and take it. "Dad?"

"Hey, kid. Listen. Go easy on everyone, all right? I know you want to help—"

"I'm the only one immune to her," I say fiercely. I catch Opal's eye. "Well, one of two people immune to her."

"I know. But you're not grown. And Opal is still teaching you to control everything. So you're where you need to be right now."

I swallow the unfairness. It would also be unfair to tell Dad that, as he has no magic, he has no business telling me what to do with mine. I'm the one who is special. I'm the one this is all about. Therefore, I am the one who has to go out there and stop her.

"I'll see you before Christmas," he says.

"Fine," I reply. "Bye for now."

I hang up the phone before he does.

"I think," Mum says loftily, holding open the kitchen door, "someone is overtired."

"All right," I say innocently. "You'd better get some rest, then, Mum."

She glares at me. I glare back. The fire in the hall crackles; we all hear it. The tea in Aunt Leanna's cup vibrates and pulses, causing her to clutch the china.

Then the phone interrupts us all once again.

"He must have forgotten something," Marley says.

I pick it up once more. "Hey, Dad. Did you—"

"Hello, sweetheart."

My throat closes and my entire body chills. It's not Dad's voice. It's a woman's voice. A powerful voice. A voice full of ancient magic and cruelty. A voice that I last heard when I was really small and my grandfather was still alive.

"Portia."

CHAPTER THREE

SIREN CALL

I say her name, and it causes everyone in the kitchen to act. Mum gasps, Leanna grabs hold of Marley, and Gran swears. If it were not so frightening to hear the siren's voice again, I would laugh. Gran never uses bad language.

Opal is instantly at my side, the only other family member who will not feel the effects of Portia's supernatural voice.

"You'll never find us," I tell the siren, trying to stop my voice from shaking. My hands are. "What do you want?"

"Well, right now, just a lovely hot bath," she says, and it's so conversational, so casual, that I almost drop the phone. "I wasn't quite ready for just how rainy your little city is. I haven't been back in such a long time."

I say nothing. I don't know what she knows, and I don't want to give her a single hint.

"Ramya." Opal speaks gently. It's the gentlest she's been since I arrived here. "Put the phone down."

I can't. I don't know why. It's not magic compelling me, it's something else. I want to say something that will hurt Portia. I want her to feel as scared as I am. I want to spit out the poisonous anger in me and see it land in her eye.

"If you don't want to come out to play with me, Ramya, that's fine," Portia goes on silkily. "There are plenty of your little Hidden Folk friends here. Some of them may even be able to help me find you."

"Why me?" I ask, and Opal makes a grab for the phone this time. "You, Ren, the fae. What's this about?"

I want her to say that it is because I am exceptional. I want to be important. I can see no other reason why she would hunt me.

If an answer was forthcoming, I would not hear it. The curly cord of the telephone snaps into two pieces, severing my connection with the siren and rendering the phone useless.

Opal pulls her hand away, having cast the little spark that caused the wire to snap.

"We don't converse with her," she finally says. "We don't negotiate. We don't argue. We do not communicate. Understood?"

"How did she get our number?" I demand. I'm too afraid to process the fear, so I mask it with anger. "You said Old Magic was protecting the house."

"Yes," Mum chimes in. "Old Magic that was cast before Alexander Graham Bell."

I've turned to ask Gran a question about her telephone when I spot something by the kitchen door. I can see some suitcases in the hall. My brain feels foggy as I stare at them. Luggage. Packed and ready to be loaded into the car.

"Are we *going* somewhere?" I finally say.

Gran and Leanna exchange a glance before Mum answers me. "Well, your grandmother and I are."

I stare at her. "And where exactly do you need to be jetting off to while we're all in danger?"

"No one owes you explanations while you're in this mood," Mum replies sternly. "We can discuss it in the morning. You need to sleep."

"No one answer any unknown numbers on your cell phones in the meantime," Gran says practically. "And, Opal, as soon as my number is changed, you're buying me a new landline."

★

MARLEY AND I ARE SHARING the tower. It's the highest part of the house: a large bedroom in the only turret. It can be a little dull up there by myself, so I'm secretly glad we will be sharing.

I'm glad he's here in general. Not that I'll tell him that.

There is only one window in the turret, and it's a deadly drop to the grass below. Clearly, despite the plentiful number of bedrooms in Gran's massive house, I was put in here for a reason.

I wait until the aunts have gone down to their own rooms, I wait until Mum says good night to me and follows them, and only once Marley and I are alone do I speak.

"We need to break out of here."

Marley is used to me by now. When we first began our quest around Edinburgh, he was a little afraid of me and my antics. I think he would sometimes wonder if I would get us both killed. Ironically, he was the one who was abducted and used as bait to lure me onto an abandoned island.

I've never asked him if he was worried I wouldn't come. I just hope he knows that I always will.

"Are we sneaking out?" he asks me, his voice a whisper.

I move to the single window, lifting up the pane. "Yes."

We both stick our heads out and stare down,

wincing in chorus as we register just how high up we really are.

"They know what they're doing," Marley murmurs, and I can hear in his voice that he's already given up.

"We can sneak out when they're asleep," I retort. "Down to the front door and out that way."

He nods and flops down onto his bed, on the other end of the large room. I sit carefully on my own, letting the quiet hang between us for a moment. Quiet after a surprisingly loud and eventful evening.

"You saw her?" I finally say.

He bends down to scratch his ankle, avoiding my stare. "Yeah."

"And?"

He sits up straight and coughs once. "And she was just like you said."

I feel validated. Sometimes, when I think about the sirens, I almost fool myself. Maybe they don't have the potential to be as bad as I imagine. Freddy is one, after all, and he is a good friend. Ren was terrible, but he could have been an outlier. Then I remind myself about what happened with Portia.

She didn't actually do anything horrendous. She only triggered the rift that kept our family apart for years. That's all.

But it's hard to articulate how she did it. How

sirens' voices can be weapons of chaos if they choose to use them.

As far as I'm aware, Portia is too clever to get her hands dirty. Ren said she had "plans," but I don't know if I want to find out what they are.

I don't want to realize that I've made up a monster in my mind. So hearing Marley say that she is exactly as I remembered . . . it's a relief. It helps.

"Portia has got fae snooping around up here," I repeat, more for myself than for Marley. "They're probably hunting for us."

"She had people with her in Edinburgh," he tells me, frowning, "but I obviously can't tell if they were magical or not."

Marley can't see through Glamour like I can, and it has always been a little bit of a sore subject between us. "What actually happened?"

Marley stares into the distance for a moment. He's far more careful with his words than I am. He is considerate. He worries over everything in life. Not just where the commas go. I can sometimes see him rehearsing every possible outcome of a situation inside his head before he's even spoken.

It must be difficult.

"I was at the school choir performance at Saint Giles," he says slowly. "It was a bad night, rain and wind and a bit of hail. We were ready to start and then Freddy appeared and—"

"Freddy?" I interrupt. "Freddy was with you?"

He fixes me with a look that is remarkably unlike him. "That piqued your interest."

I scowl and make a noise of derision. "Shut up, you just surprised me."

I reach under my pillow and haul a bright pink laptop out from underneath it. I sit it on my knees and open it, clicking on my inbox. Dad bought the laptop for me before he relocated to London for work, but I spend most of my time on it emailing Freddy. He writes an update from Edinburgh each morning and I reply every night before bed.

"He didn't know this ambush was coming," I say. When Marley says nothing back, I snap, "Marley. He didn't."

"Well, fine, if you say so. He did get me out of there, but he knew something was about to go down. Without a doubt."

"Well, what about our mums?"

Marley considers this and then nods. "They were waiting outside. They knew too. At least that something was about to happen."

"I told Freddy to get straight to the three of you at the first sign of trouble," I tell Marley, pointedly and smugly. "And it appears he did."

"But who tipped him off? Plus, he stayed behind. What if he's with them? He's one of them, if you recall."

“There is no ‘them,’ ” I say. I say it because I need to say it to myself every day. If I have to hear it, then so does he. “And Freddy’s our friend.”

“He’s your friend,” Marley corrects me. “If ‘friend’ is even the right word.”

“Oh, be quiet,” I mumble, typing furiously on the computer. “I’m checking in with him. Shall I thank him for you?”

Marley rolls his eyes but nods.

“We need to scout the area, see if any fae are camped out nearby.”

“That drop will kill me,” Marley says, staring at the open window. “You too, if you can’t—” He stops himself, but not before I understand his meaning.

“I can fly.”

“I know you can,” he says quickly. “I’ve seen it. It’s just . . . Mum mentioned—”

“I just don’t do it without Opal there,” I say. I’m not sure why I’m so defensive. “It’s dangerous, I’m still learning. I just—”

“It’s all right,” Marley interjects softly. “It’s fine. It’s more than I can do, obviously. I know it must be hard. It’s fine, I just meant . . . I just meant we shouldn’t test your abilities by jumping out of a window.”

Silence. Then we both burst into a fit of giggles. I rock back and forth, shaking, and Marley does the snorting thing he does when something has truly tickled him. When the laughter subsides, I glance at the bedroom door.

"Come on," I say, with a voice full of excitement. We're back together. Back on a quest and back out in the world of witchery and Hidden Folk. "Let's try the front way."

I yank the bedroom door open while Marley grabs his favorite flashlight. Both of us stumble to a grinding halt as we spot a figure sitting at the top of the stairs, with a book and a glass of water.

"Oh, yes," Opal says, her voice dripping with mockery. "I wondered how long it would be before you tried sneaking out."

"We're just getting snacks," Marley says. The lie is pretty impressive coming from him; I'm usually the one who covers our tracks. "Dinner was a bit stressful."

Opal rises to her full height, crosses her arms, and locks eyes with Marley. He visibly gulps but tries to maintain an innocent expression as he looks back at her.

"Marley," she says slowly. "I'm sorry you're hungry. What can I bring up from the pantry for you? You and your flashlight?"

There is a challenge in her voice, one that neither of us can misinterpret.

"Gran says not to eat food upstairs," I say, trying to sound casual instead of suspicious. "So we'll just—"

I make to go down the staircase, but she steps in front of me.

"If you seriously think," she says matter-of-factly, "that you're getting out of this house in the middle of the night, while fae are in the area and sirens are plotting who even knows what, then you are suffering from some incredibly strong delusions."

"Listen," I reply, all attempts at playing sweet and delightful now gone. "If the grown-ups want to sit around and wait for something to happen, that's on you. But I'm going to find out whatever it is the fae are sniffing around for."

"You!" barks Opal. "It's probably you. Or haven't you worked that one out yet?"

I try to hide my delight. I really am special, then. "Why me? You're more powerful than I am. Every creature from here to Edinburgh has come skulking around, trying to get an audience with the Heartbroken Witch."

"Yes," Opal says. "Which is why I stay indoors. Don't think for a moment they're not gunning for me, too."

"So let's blast them!" I say, every atom of me animated and alive. "Your magic and mine, we can do it!"

However, despite my enthusiasm, her face remains passive and almost empty. She regards me. Considering me.

"I'm not really into 'blasting' people," she finally says, still watching me steadily. Her eyes are tinged with just the slightest shade of judgment. "Sorry."

I feel a cold trickle of shame, which needles into embarrassment and then rage. "You blasted Ren. You turned him to stone."

Marley flinches. Opal does not.

"I did," she acknowledges. "Because I had run out of options. We, as of right now, are full of options."

"If we attack them, they won't have a chance to attack us!"

The words stand with the three of us, like a fourth person.

"You know what's funny, Ramya," Opal breathes, her voice raspy and tired, "that's exactly what they're thinking too."

It's a blow. A stinging spit in the face. "That's not fair."

She does not react. "Go to bed. Both of you. Stay there. I'm conserving magic at the moment. As much as possible. If I have to waste some of it getting the two of you out of trouble, I'll be very angry."

My pain is briefly tabled for curiosity. "Why? What spell are you working on?"

She does not answer my question. "Go to sleep. There's lots to discuss in the morning."

She moves a few steps down the staircase and sits once more, lifting her book and returning to her reading. It's a clear dismissal. Marley inches back into our room in the tower, defeated. I stay.

"I just meant," I say shakily, "I just—"

"I know what you meant," she responds, not glancing up from the book.

I cannot make myself move. "You're making me feel like a bad person."

At first, she says nothing, but I can see that her eyes have stopped scanning the pages.

"We can get out of a lot of guilt by telling ourselves we only hurt someone because they were the wrong sort of person," she finally says quietly. "That we're the main character and they're someone who went off script to play the villain."

I bristle and throb, fully awake and teeming with angry energy. "She is a villain. You didn't see her like I did."

"When you were very small? Good judge of character, were you?"

"Yes!" I bellow. "I saw through Ren before any of you, remember? And you haven't met Portia."

"Actually, I have."

The words stop me in my tracks. "You have?"

"A long time ago."

I close my mouth and try to regain some control within the conversation, but she speaks again.

"There was a reason she was at your house that night, Ramya."

"It was a party."

"And who gets invited to parties?"

I shrug. "Family. Friends."

"Precisely."

Before I can ask some much-needed follow-up questions, she flicks her wrist toward our bedroom door. It opens, and the expression she gives me is one not to be challenged. She is done with me for the night.

For once, I don't push. I step back inside my room.

"Good night, Ramya," she says to my back, her voice finally devoid of that cold touch.

I don't respond.

Marley is sitting on his bed, watching me as I close the door behind me.

"Shall we just scout during the day?" he stage-whispers.

I hardly hear him. I'm staring at the still-open window, its curtains fluttering in the winter wind.

"Marley," I murmur, my voice no louder than the creak of the floorboard I step upon as I move farther into the room, toward the moonlight. "Look."

We both go to the window.

"How?" Marley gasps. "How has it . . . ?"

Standing tall outside the house, in a place where nothing stood before, is the oak tree from the front garden. Taller than it was, and now next to our room.

CHAPTER FOUR

ALONA

"It moved," I say. "It keeps moving! I didn't imagine it." I can sense Marley's bewilderment.

"The tree?"

"Yeah," I answer, sliding the windowpane all the way up and letting the winter cold slither inside. "It was around at the front of the house when you arrived. Remember? Now it's here. And bigger."

Being able to see through magical Glamour is definitely a gift, but sometimes it's lonely. When you're the only one who can see something that wants to be hidden, it's difficult. Marley and I view the world through entirely different lenses. It frustrates and isolates both of us sometimes. Yet Marley always tries to understand what I'm seeing, and never tells me I'm insane.

Which is all I need, really.

I glance back at the bedroom door, making sure it's shut tight. Then I swing myself out onto the windowsill and grab hold of the nearest, and most sturdy-seeming, branch. The oak tree has plenty, so I start to move.

"What are you doing?" gasps Marley.

He is right to be horrified. I'm dyspraxic. It's a learning difficulty that affects coordination, speech, and motor skills. I'm perhaps not best suited for climbing up or down massive trees that are as high as a tower.

Yet that is exactly what I'm doing.

I shinny my way toward the trunk of the tree, careful not to look down. Instead, I throw Marley a glance and jerk my head toward the oak. "Come on. It's fine. It's also our only way down."

He more than hesitates. He is incredibly skeptical.

"Wait," I suddenly say.

"I wasn't doing anything," he replies, still gingerly eyeing up the tree. "What?"

"Grab my bag. It's on my bed."

He vanishes for a moment and returns with a tote bag I bought from a bookshop in Portobello Market. It has Grandpa's book inside it. My book now, I suppose. He left it to me via a mysterious stranger, and my job is to use it to catalogue as many Hidden Folk as I can.

That mission hasn't ended just because a siren has arrived in Edinburgh. If anything, it's more urgent. If we're all going up against an ancient enemy like the sirens, we're going to need numbers. We're going to need support.

Marley holds out the tote bag and, for a moment, makes to throw it to me. I glare at him, disbelief scrawled across my face.

"Are you serious, Marley? You think I'm going to catch that?"

"Use your magic."

I fidget, adjusting my position on the tree. "No. You carry it."

He stares at me and I look away. There is a pause long enough to tell me he's considering whether or not to press the matter, but he decides not to. He swings the tote over his shoulder and shadows my path along the branch of the tree.

"What's wrong with good old-fashioned bed-sheets tied together?" he mumbles, reaching me next to the trunk.

"We're too high up for that," I reply, wincing as I take a quick peek down. I need to be careful about my route. "Follow me slowly, and if you hear a crack, don't grab whatever I've just grabbed."

"Obviously."

I start my descent. It's clumsy and haphazard, but I don't lose my grip. I can hear Marley slowly descending behind me.

"If you do fall, just use your powers," he says pointedly.

I grimace. "Shut up."

"I mean it. What's the use of flight if you can't use it to save yourself—and your favorite cousin—from a broken neck?"

"I said be quiet."

I'm distracted enough to misjudge a hand placement. My fingers slip. I let out a noise of fear.

Marley catches me. Our palms grip together in silence, in the dark, and the unspoken question sits between both of us.

Why can't I use my powers?

Neither of us speaks as my feet, then hands find their way back to solid branches and then the ground. When we make it to the grass, I shush him, not sure if all of the family are asleep. We need to get away from the house. He silently returns my tote bag with the book, and I point wordlessly toward the loch. He nods once.

We start to move.

Once we're away from the house, I let out a puff of air.

"What kind of Hidden Folk live in these parts?" Marley asks.

I sit down by the water, calmed by its presence, and I flip open the book. I've made some preliminary notes on what I've seen since arriving at Loch Ness. "More than I've found, I know that."

"Such as?"

"Blue Men."

"What?"

"Blue Men of the Minch. And whatever you do, don't call them kelpies. It really offends them. They kinda seem like blue versions, but don't bring it up."

"Sure," Marley says sardonically. "The next time I'm chatting with some Blue Men of the Minch, I'll be sure to keep any comparisons to kelpies on the down-low."

He's joking because he has never quite recovered from the kelpies. They are strange, alluring yet terrifying water horses that will save your life or end it depending on their mood. They worked with me to save Marley from Inchkeith island, but he has never been able to relax around their watery manes and cold eyes.

I like them. Everything about them is designed to frighten and repel me, but I like them. I can't help it.

"What else?" Marley asks, reading my notes on

the Blue Men. He turns the page and frowns as he sees that it's blank.

"Yeah," I say, a little embarrassed. "I've been a bit busy."

Before he can challenge me by saying "With what?," as I've clearly got no magical improvements to show for this alleged busyness, I change the subject.

"Fae were seen snooping around," I reiterate. "I doubt they're searching for me."

"If Opal thinks—"

"I know they're not," I say. I cannot tell him how I know, only that I do. "This place . . . it's quieter than Edinburgh. It may seem emptier or simpler or even completely deserted. But it's not. It's teeming with magic."

"Well." Marley peers around at the vast loch and the trees surrounding it. "I wouldn't know about that."

"This place is made up of so much water," I say excitedly. "That's how I know. It's full of new things to find. And whatever they're hunting, it's around here somewhere."

We stare out at the water. Something hoots in the distance. The loch is so still, like glass. A great mirror that allows you a reflection, but not a glimpse at anything deeper beneath.

Marley settles in front of the water's edge and gestures out at the vastness. "Do you think—"

"No."

He groans and raises an eyebrow at me. "Ramya. It might just mean—"

"The fae are not up here," I say dourly, "to hunt down a manufactured tourist trap. Something that does not exist. Something that locals MADE UP to lure people here so that they would spend money. And by the way, most of the living locals hate that silly story. It was started by some chancer hundreds of years ago, and they're stuck with it."

Marley shrugs his shoulders. "No smoke without fire."

Before I can even realize I'm doing it, I hold out my hand, and a fierce, crackling flame appears in my palm. Marley curses and leaps away, his eyes glued to it.

"Look, Marley," I say dryly. "No smoke. Just fire."

"Since when can you do fire?" he breathes, still staring at the tiny flame.

I close my palm into a fist and the embers die. "I can't. Not really."

"That did *not* seem like 'not really.' "

"I can't do things off the cuff the way Opal can," I say, a little too bitterly. "It flares up when I do. But . . . I don't know. It's hard to control."

I know he has a thousand burning questions, but he's sensitive enough not to throw them at me right now.

I gaze back out at the water, unnerved as ever by how still it can be. Even thinking about how deep it is makes me shiver.

"There is something in there," I say. "But it's not the Loch Ness Monster. It's not some fairy tale. None of this has been like the stories."

I sit down beside him.

"You can see the moon in the water," Marley says absentmindedly while I slide the book back into my tote bag. I glance over to the spot he's looking at, and I freeze.

"That's not the moon," I murmur.

It certainly is a light, but it's not a reflection. It moves closer, still under the water. I instinctively shuffle backward, sitting back on my heels. Marley leans a little closer, almost hypnotized by the shine.

"It's eyes," I say. I can hear my own fear, but it doesn't seem to bother Marley. "Marley, it's—"

A pair of eyes glow beneath the water and then a head slowly breaks the surface. It's a pale, gaunt face, with eyes like saucers full of stars. It seems like a woman, with seaweed hair stuck to her cheeks.

I can make out a tail instead of legs. But she is no mermaid. No scales, no shimmer, no fish tail.

Instead of legs, she has an otter's lower body, brown fur matching her hair.

Her eyes are locked on Marley as she reaches a webbed hand out slowly.

To my horror, he reaches back.

"No!" I yell, grabbing hold of his shoulders and pulling him away from the water. But the creature has a grip. It reveals sharp, jagged teeth and starts trying to pull him beneath the surface.

I'm about to attempt another fire spell when something interrupts the three of us, something none of us were expecting.

The creature is rushed by what appears to be a horde of leaves. Harsh winter leaves all flying like a hive of bees. They lambaste the creature's face, causing it to shriek in surprise and let go of Marley's hand. I don't hesitate. I yank him backward, dragging him right up onto the bank.

Only once we are safely free from the water's edge, and away from the strange creature, does the small tornado made of leaves relent. It disappears so speedily, my eyes can't track it. The creature in the water hisses and spits but disappears beneath the surface, submerged and invisible once again.

Marley and I both pant out terrified breaths, glancing around to try to see what saved both of our skins.

"Were those leaves?" he chokes out.

"That's what I thought," I reply. "You were just saved from a gross, watery death by . . . some leaves."

I spot my bag down by the water and start moving toward it. Marley grabs my elbow and stops me.

"That thing might come back."

"No offense," I say, slipping free of his grip, "but I was fine. You were the one offering yourself up on a platter."

"I couldn't look away from it."

I can hear the hurt and loathing in his voice, and I instantly feel horrible. Despite being frightened, he's probably thinking of Ren. Thinking of what it feels like to be at the mercy of a vicious supernatural creature.

I'm trying to think of something comforting and helpful to say when I see her standing on the beach.

A girl. Or what appears to be a girl. Our age, our height, with pale green hair that falls to her hips and long eyelashes that are exactly the same shade of emerald. Her skin seems to be made of patches of tree bark.

There is healthy moss on her elbows and ankles. Her clothes are not even clothes, not really. They are leaves all melded together to create the rudimentary shape of a dress.

Only her eyes are human, but not in their color, a bright shade of orange that is warm and volcanic.

There's an ancientness about her, which is bizarre when she seems as young as we do.

The orange eyes with green lashes are fixed on me, and I'm nervous all over again.

"Marley?" I ask quietly, never glancing away from this strange girl. "Do you see her?"

Marley nods shakily. "Yes."

"All of her?"

"Skin like a tree, green hair?" he says, like it is a question. He is checking to see if we are staring at the same creature. One with no Glamour. "I can see her."

"I want you to see me."

Marley and I both startle at the sound of her voice. She sounds like one of us, like any other student from our school.

Who happens to be supernatural.

"I'm a dryad," she goes on, cheerful and unafraid of us. She moves closer, fluid and graceful, like a leaf moving in the breeze. "I saved you from the ceasg."

She smiles, a candid grin. A *KEE-ask,* she had called that thing. Marley and I look at each other and then quickly away again, neither of us exactly sure of what to do with the strange new creature we are faced with—even though we have met with a great many strange Hidden Folk, thanks to our recent quest.

“Thank you,” I eventually manage to force out.

It is obviously the correct thing to say, as she lights up all over and moves even closer, cocking her head to one side as she takes the two of us in.

“You’re welcome. I’m Alona. Can I be in that little book, please? I did help you escape from the big house.”

I gape at her. “You?”

She laughs, delighted by my surprise. Then, before Marley and I even have a chance to process, she transforms in an instant into a handful of leaves.

Then, into an oak tree.

CHAPTER FIVE

AN OLD, STRANGE FRIEND

"You can turn into a tree?"

I feel a little slow as I say the words, but it's been an eventful day and I'm slightly overwhelmed. The tree morphs into leaves and then back into Alona, the girl with green hair and moss between her toes. She does a cartwheel, still utterly delighted by our stunned reactions.

"I'm a dryad," she repeats, in a tone that suggests we ought to know exactly what that means. "I want to be in your little book. It's a book of Hidden Folk, isn't it? I can't really Glamour, but I'd still like—"

"You were the tree by our window," I interrupt, still trying to understand her sudden entrance into our story. "The one we climbed down?"

She nods, eyes wide and alert. "You said you needed to get out, so . . ."

"So you moved from the front garden to our window?" Marley asks, his voice frayed at the edges. He is as overwhelmed as I am. "You were the tree."

Alona blinks and puzzles over the two of us for a moment. "I am not sure what is not making sense for you both."

"Sorry," I say. "It's been . . . a day. And we really should be going."

I throw Marley a wordless expression and he nods, almost imperceptibly. We start to edge back up toward the trees, no longer eager to flee the house.

"Oh, I see," Alona says, a little despondently. "But how are you going to get back in without me?"

I can see by Marley's body language that the realization has hit both of us at the same moment. The tree will no longer be next to the window.

"He said you can fly," Alona adds, addressing me. She crouches low and gazes up at me, as if she's completely fascinated. I find it just a bit too eerie. "Can you?"

I'm not supposed to speak to anyone outside the family about my powers. I should deny it. I should laugh and say she overheard us joking.

"You're a witch."

She speaks the words with wonder. I like the way she says it. I have not been feeling that attached to the word lately, sometimes even anxious about using it, so I like hearing it. I sometimes don't feel I have the right to use the word "witch." Opal has the right. Mum has the right. Leanna has the right.

I don't know if I do.

"I'm learning," I say finally.

"And the things you write about in that little book? That's part of the learning?"

"Well, sort of," I say. "It's kind of like a glossary. Of all the different Hidden Folk. My grandfather started it."

"Are there dryads?"

"No," Marley says, nervously looking her up and down. "You're the first."

She claps her hands and falls into another crouch. She gestures toward the book. "Put me in it. I can also tell you about the ceasg."

"That demonic mermaid thing?" Marley says, shuddering.

"It was like an otter crossed with a human," I muse, pulling the book toward me and obediently opening it. "What is it?"

"Water dweller. Likes to drown people. For sport and for food. That's about it, really. It usually tries to lure people under. Less splashing about that way. It must have been a junior one that we saw, otherwise it wouldn't have been that bothered by someone like me."

The image of her hive of leaves attacking the ceasg floods my mind, and I wish for the millionth time that I were an artist. Then I could draw it. "Thanks. I'll put that down once we get home."

"And then me?"

"Maybe."

She pouts and suddenly transforms into one singular leaf. It makes both of us start in surprise. She transforms back, laughing loudly and joyously.

"That is a good trick," mutters Marley.

"I'm still learning too," Alona giggles, gauging my face for a reaction. She wants me to laugh as well. I know it. "Just like you."

I study her, still not sure what I think. I don't make friends that easily. Even if they can impress me by turning into a tree.

"I can show you both all kinds of things around these parts, if you like," she says with openness and enthusiasm.

I shove the book into my bag and start heading back to the house, knowing both of them will follow. "What things?"

"Hidden lands, secret places."

It's the piece of this quest I can never resist. I stop walking and hesitate.

"No," Marley says firmly. "We've done enough tonight, Ramya."

I try to be endearing. "What's one more thing, then?"

"No," he says, refusing to be persuaded. "My head hurts and I was almost drowned by a killer . . . whatever that thing was."

"Ceasg," Alona and I say simultaneously.

"Fine. Well, it tried to drown me or eat me, and it didn't even have the courtesy to Glamour itself, so I'm going to be having nightmares about that for some time. I'd like to go home now."

"All right, all right, relax. We're going home." I still don't move, though. I'm watching Alona. Taking in this strange nature girl with her green hair, bright eyes, and earthy apparel. "How old are you?"

"Oh." She thinks for a moment, scratching her left ankle with the big toe of her right foot. Her feet are dirty from the woodland floor. "I was made a couple of years ago. In spring, I think. It was warm."

"What a nice story," Marley says quickly. "You can tell us all about it when we next meet. Later. After tonight. Because we're going to bed. Good night."

Alona laughs again, clearly finding Marley's cantankerousness amusing. The giggle suddenly dies, however, and her entire face darkens as her eyes lock on something behind my cousin and me. She stumbles backward and transforms instantly into a tree.

I frown and turn, steeling my nerves for whatever is there.

I exhale and release all my fear, amazed at what I see. "You."

The Stranger is standing at the front gate of our house. He wears black, as he always does, with a bright teal pocket square in his jacket. I always remember little details about him when we're face to face again, but when we're apart it's impossible. He evades memory. He is impossible to describe. It's a strange sort of spell he has about him. I don't know his name, and he always brushes that off, stating that he has too many.

He's the one who really changed the direction of my life. I was walking through the Old Town of Edinburgh when I saw a little statue of a dog leap down from its podium and trot along Candlemaker Row, into the Stranger's bookshop. He was the one who gave me the book. He was the one who told me about the Hidden Folk. He was the one who started me on my grandfather's quest.

"Lovely to see you again, Ramya."

I turn back to Alona, who remains transformed. The tree stands still and steady; no passerby would believe it to be enchanted. A dryad in plain sight.

"Wish I could say the same."

He laughs. "What have I done?"

Marley takes a step forward, addressing the

Stranger. "You never just show up without a reason. So what is it this time?"

"Look how jaded the two of you have become."

His power is probably stronger than that of anyone I know, even stronger than Aunt Opal's. He feels otherworldly in a way that makes me intrigued but also nervous. It's as if he's part of something so much bigger than all of us. That's how he knows so many things.

"Portia's hunting for something in the area."

He says the words seriously. He is not joking with us now.

"Is it Ramya?" Marley asks directly. "Is that why she came to Edinburgh?"

The Stranger watches me, and I watch him back. "Why do you think Portia is after you, Ramya?"

"She rocked up with a squad of henchmen in Edinburgh," Marley says indignantly, and I'm surprised at how animated he is. He seems different tonight. "She also called the house. She's not exactly subtle."

"No need to bite my head off," the Stranger says serenely, picking at an invisible piece of lint on his jacket. "I know you two are used to dealing with sirens."

"Yeah, we only just got away from the last one, no thanks to you," Marley mutters.

The Stranger has not glanced away from me once.

"Ramya can take care of her own affairs. Can't you?"

I bristle. "Yes."

"Why ask for help when you can do everything yourself?"

I scowl. "Exactly."

We stare each other down, just as we did in Avizandum—his bookshop on Candlemaker Row, the place where we last met.

"She's hunting more than just you," the Stranger finally says. His words chill me.

I can feel Marley glancing at me. Even though she is hidden in her other form, I can tell Alona is listening nervously. I can just feel the energy behind me, mingled with her fear of the Stranger.

Maybe I should be afraid too. Maybe it's very unwise to be unafraid of him.

"Don't forget how we met," the Stranger says, nodding toward the tote bag on my shoulder. "What your grandfather wanted you to do."

"Document the Hidden Folk, I know," I reply. "But we were almost eaten by one just now."

"Aw, no," the Stranger says cheerfully. "She just wanted to drown you both for sport. Neither of you would make a very appetizing meal for her."

Marley makes a small noise of distress, and I shake my head in disgust. "What is Portia searching for?"

"You never know, Ramya," the Stranger says, beginning to fade away before our eyes. "You might find it before Portia does. Better watch where you step."

He vanishes. As soon as he's gone, Alona returns.

Her bare feet move toward us as she stares at the spot where the Stranger stood a moment ago. The chill I had starts to disappear, and I can't hold on to the serious feelings I had while he was here.

"He's weird like that," I say flippantly.

"He's not human," Alona says, reaching down to touch where his feet were. "Not Hidden Folk, either."

"No," I agree, heading back to the house once more. "He's annoying."

Alona walks with us both until we're beneath our bedroom window again. I turn to her, a little awkwardly.

"Um." I jerk my head up toward the window. "Would you mind—"

"Of course!" Alona says enthusiastically.

Her transformation is quite amazing to see when I truly pay attention. It's smooth, no sound of bones breaking to form bark or anything ripping, just the sinuous movement that turns girl into tree with a seamless ripple. As a small oak stands before us, Marley and I carefully climb on. Only once we are holding on tight to the branches does the tree shoot up.

We both make noises of surprise as it rises toward the sky, returning to the height it was when we first climbed down.

As we clamber into our quiet bedroom, I turn to stare at the now stationary oak.

"Thanks," I whisper, knowing the dryad can hear me. "See you at the same time tomorrow."

I'm so tired, I can feel myself falling into sleep as soon as my head is on the pillow, but I'm watching Alona as I slip away.

A dryad. Grandpa would have loved that.

CHAPTER SIX

WITCHES AND WELLS

"You two are up to something, I can tell."

Aunt Leanna says so to my cousin and me as we eat breakfast. Both of us are a little drowsy after last night's adventure, but we obviously do not reveal what happened. As far as the grown-ups are concerned, we spent all night in our room. Disgruntled but definitely safe and away from any Hidden Folk in Loch Ness.

The oak tree was gone when we woke up. The grown-ups haven't noticed that, either.

Aunt Leanna is the only one here with us in the breakfast nook, and she's making sure to scrape lots of egg and sausages onto our plates.

"All this food will just make me more tired," Marley complains.

"I'll have yours, then," I say, picking up his plate and letting some of his breakfast slide gracelessly onto mine.

Aunt Opal enters the room. She eyes us steadily, clearly aware that something has happened.

Reading minds is not one of her many gifts, though.

I think.

"Anything you want to tell me, Ramya?"

I try to smile innocently up at Opal, wondering if this is just like when the teachers at school know someone has done something wrong but they don't know who it is. They do the whole "come forward and make it easier on yourself" speech, trying to scare the culprit into confessing. When, in actual fact, they have no proof.

They never caught me drawing rude things on the French teacher's desk, so I'm not falling for it now.

"I slept really well," I tell her, taking a large bite of scrambled egg. "Thank you."

She surprises me by laughing under her breath before she moves to the teapot. She pours an enormous cup of tea and then joins us in the breakfast nook.

"What are today's plans, then?" asks Leanna brightly, using her own knife and fork to put some more mushrooms onto Marley's plate.

"I think," Opal says between sips of tea, wincing

at the sunlight pouring into the kitchen, "it's time to get back to magic."

Marley looks at me in excited glee, but I narrow my eyes. "You said last night I had to do schoolwork."

"You do."

"And you said we wouldn't start up again. What's changed?"

"Well, with fae stalking about and a siren calling the house, I think it would be wise," she snaps, glaring at me.

"That's what I've been saying—"

"You're getting what you want," she says curtly. "Now don't push it."

Aunt Leanna reaches across to gently tug my earlobe. "You are such a cheeky one! You're just like your aunt."

Opal and I both roll our eyes at that. I turn to the kitchen door and frown as I realize that the luggage from last night is gone.

"What happened to the bags?"

Leanna's smile slips, and Opal glances behind her at the door to the hall.

"The suitcases," I say. "Where are they?"

When no one says anything, I take in the quiet of the house for the first time. No sound of a bath being drawn upstairs or someone moving about in another room.

"Where are Mum and Gran?"

Opal pushes her teacup away from her, and Leanna stares down at her own empty plate. I watch my two aunts say nothing for a good thirty seconds before Opal finally releases a sigh and speaks.

"They left very early this morning, on important business."

Marley suddenly appears to be very hungry after all. He starts to shovel food into his mouth, all while avoiding my eyes. He couldn't have known they were planning to go, but what he does know is my temper.

"I see," I say icily. "So that's why witch lessons are back on the menu. They've made a run for it and you feel guilty."

"They have not 'made a run for it,' " Opal scoffs. "Your grandmother has her own work to deal with, and your mum is going to London to join your father. They can hold the fort there."

I'm not being told the whole story, but when have I ever been allowed that privilege?

"Your mum checked in on you before she left this morning," Leanna says gently. "But she didn't want to wake you. She has such a soft spot for you when you're sleeping soundly and quietly." We all stare at her, even Opal.

"I didn't mean it like that," she adds hastily. "It's hard to explain; it's a maternal thing."

"Well, I'm so grateful to both of you for tolerating me while I'm awake," I snipe. "So grateful. Can we get back to flying now, please?"

"Not with that attitude," Opal retorts.

One thing Opal has taught me about magic is that emotion can heighten or hinder it. I've flown well two times in my life, and they were both very emotional moments. My overstimulation aided me in flight. It's not a healthy way to use magic, though. Opal took a long break from witchcraft when she was depressed.

When magic is blue, it's not for you.

A member of the Hidden Folk said that to me once. In the Grassmarket, back in Edinburgh.

I miss them. Murrey. Erica. Freddy.

It's so lonely up here.

★

THE SUN IS DAZZLING BUT cold today as Opal leads me down to the water's edge. I feel slightly nervy as we approach, but Marley is back at the house with Aunt Leanna. I don't need to haul him to safety, should another creature from the deep attempt to steal him.

"They say in battle, your armor is more important than your weapon," Opal tells me as we stand with ten feet of ground between us by the cold and quiet loch. "So it's time to cover shielding."

I kick a pebble. "Can't we start with blasting spells?"

"No."

"You think lots of people will try to blast me?"

"Without a doubt. I've considered it three times today and it's not even noon."

She smiles softly after she says it, though. I do too. "Breathe with your diaphragm," she says, once the moment has passed. "Concentrate. Connect with your core and trust your instincts."

I move my stance. I push my feet into the earth. "Ready."

She takes a moment and then there is a flash, too quick for me to even see it. It hits me and knocks me backward. I curse and get back up at once. I open my mouth, prickling at the embarrassment of it.

"Don't make excuses," she says swiftly, before I can speak. "Don't be angry, just be better."

"Fine," I growl. "Do it again."

She doesn't wait this time; she throws a spell at me with rapid speed. I fling my hand up to push it away, the way you would if someone had thrown a tennis ball at you. I only just catch the spell, redirecting it, but barely.

"All right," Opal says. "An improvement."

"Do it again," I repeat. Determined. "Come on."

We continue. When I react too quickly or try to outsmart her, I miss. The spell knocks me down. I get back up and try again. Another spell. Another fall.

If there is one thing I know as a dyspraxic girl, it's that staying down is not an option. People expect you to. They sometimes want you to. So I always get back up. If I have to fail one hundred times, I will. I don't care how many people see me do it. They're going to see me succeed, too.

I hate when other people treat my learning difficulty as if it's something to overcome, when it's not. It's part of my brain. The same brain that gives me all my gifts. No, it's not being dyspraxic that I have to overcome. There is nothing wrong with that. It's other people. The thing I have to overcome is them.

Whoever "them" is. It often changes. Sometimes it's the sirens. Sometimes it's a substitute teacher at school. Sometimes it's my own parents.

Sometimes it's me.

I always have an enemy to fight. So I get back up.

Overcoming "them" has become my focus. The shape may shift, the object of my attention might differ, but I don't stop. I can accept being an underdog, but I will never accept anyone treating me as anything less than anyone else.

"Hit me again," I say, a little out of breath but steady on my feet. Opal considers me.

Then fires another spell.

This time I blast it back. It hits her square in the

sternum and she stumbles a little before righting herself. I feel a flash of guilt before remembering that this is a training session.

She grins at me. "Good."

I bend down to pick up my beret. It fell from my head with the power of the spell. I hold it thoughtfully for a moment before I put it on.

"It's getting a little small for you," Opal says quietly. "That beret."

It's the one he gave me. So long ago now. "It's fine."

She opens her mouth but says nothing, glancing out at the water instead. "He loved this place."

I look up, hungry for more. "Grandpa?"

"Yeah. He loved the quiet. I think he could sense it, too. The magic. In his own way. He could feel how many creatures lurk about up here."

I touch my beret. "Even if he couldn't see them?"

"We can feel lots of things we can't see," she says pensively. "Especially in a place like this."

I gaze out at the still, deceptive water. The loch that appears to be so quiet and yet, last night, released a killer mermaid upon us. "I suppose."

"Witch!"

The word is shouted by a man from farther down the bank of the loch, and it's not called out in anger or hatred. Rather, with delight.

Opal and I turn to see who it is. A middle-aged

man with gray hair is bounding toward us, his enthusiastic energy infectious. I watch Opal's shoulders sag, possibly in relief.

"Angus," she says, her voice a mixture of fondness and exasperation. "Can the museum spare you?"

"Oh, of course, it's winter. Not our season. I'm so glad I caught you, Opal!"

"Angus, this is my niece, Ramya," Opal says nonchalantly. "Ramya, this is Angus. He runs the visitor center back in Drumnadrochit."

The older man shakes my hand with ferocious gusto. "I know your grandparents well! And your aunt and her sisters, of course. How do you do!"

"Hello," I say, vibrato in my voice from the power of his greeting. "Nice to meet you."

"Did your aunt tell you about the beastie of the lake?"

"No!" I cry, and Opal inhales.

"Because there isn't one, Angus," she says wearily. "I won't stop you fooling boatloads of tourists in the summer, but you can't bring those tales around here."

"Your family taught me all about magic," Angus tells me happily. "Your grandfather and I would have long chats about it on this very bank while this one practiced enchantments."

I turn to Opal, but she's staring off into the distance, waiting for the conversation to end.

"You really think there's a monster in the loch?" I ask, wondering if the fearsome creature that almost captured Marley is behind all the myths and stories.

"I know there is," Angus responds triumphantly. Opal sighs, but he ignores her. "Too many strange occurrences. Too many accounts from the odd traveler, all of which match up. There is most certainly something in there."

"Did you come all this way to spread rumors, Angus?" Opal asks.

"No, I came to see if Isabelle is coming to bridge this Friday. I couldn't get through over the phone."

"She's"—Opal glances quickly at me and then away again, speaking with slow intensity—"out of the country on important business. If you need any help at the bridge club, then you can come to me. All right?"

"Ah," Angus says, understanding entering his face. "I see. Very good."

I frown, a little confused.

"This your first time in Loch Ness, young lady?" asks Angus affably.

"I was here when I was very little," I admit, "but this is my first time back."

"Well, Angus knows just about everything a non-magical person can know about these parts," Opal tells me warmly.

"And I get the rest from the Hidden Folk," Angus

adds, seeming very pleased with that fact. "They know they don't have to Glamour around me. I hear all sorts. Did you know that this loch is said to be connected underwater to another? To Loch Maree! Queen Victoria herself visited there, and they are believed to have their very own monster, too."

"People love to make up fairy tales about monsters of the deep," Opal says wryly. "When they have real ones on their very doorstep."

"Another loch with a whole other monster?" I say teasingly. "Wow. Shame Loch Ness gets all the attention."

"It is, rather," Angus agrees, either missing my sarcasm or choosing to ignore it.

"We're a little busy at the moment, Angus," Opal says, not impolitely. "I'll drop in on you if I get the chance."

"There is, uh, something else," Angus says guardedly.

Opal arches an eyebrow. "Yes?"

"A few Hidden Folk have been in my cellar for a dram of whiskey and . . . well . . . there's been some talk."

"Of fae?" I ask, perhaps a little prematurely.

Both adults stare at me. Angus is shocked. "Fae?"

"Some were spotted in the area," Opal says hurriedly, glowering at me. "Lock your doors and trust your gut, it should be fine."

"Well. That's . . . anyhow. Hidden Folk have been in, regular folk as well, if I'm being honest."

"And?" Opal prompts when he looks unsure.

His face is pale, and all his good humor is gone as he stares at my aunt. "People are saying they've seen a ghost."

Opal's entire face hardens. "Nonsense."

"I don't think so, lass. Their expressions . . . even the Hidden Folk. If you saw them, you wouldn't call them liars."

"No, perhaps not," Opal says. "Just fools. Fooled by the wind and the moonlight and centuries of silly tales. There is no such thing as ghosts, Angus. You know that."

Something saddens in his eyes, and he nods. "Well. That's what the talk of the town is, anyway. I won't disturb you."

We watch him turn to leave. "Angus?" Opal calls after him.

He turns back at us. "Aye?"

Opal pauses before she speaks. "I mean it. There really is no such thing. They've misunderstood."

Angus nods dazedly, but he doesn't seem convinced. He walks away.

He is already halfway back to the nearest village before I can ask what unspoken understanding the two of them just shared.

"Come on," Opal says briskly. "Let's take a walk."

She leads me in the other direction, and he's out of sight by the time I catch up to her.

"How do you know there isn't a creature in there?" I ask her, just trying to match her long strides.

"There are sturgeon in that water," she says plainly. "Kelpies when the weather is poor. Blue Men if they're migrating. And perhaps the odd ceasg."

I flinch at the name. Reliving last night, with the shining eyes in the water and the vicious teeth.

"But no Loch Ness Monster," Opal asserts.

"What's a ceasg?" I ask innocently.

"Hope you never find out."

Too late.

We walk through the trees between the loch and the road. I try to walk exactly where she does, making sure I keep up.

"And you're sure there is no such thing—"

She reels around before I can even finish my question. She kneels down in front of me so that our eyes are level. She seems desperate for a moment, vulnerable in a way I did not anticipate.

"Ramya, listen to me. I know recently there has been a lot of change. Vampires, fae, Hidden Folk, and sirens. But believe me. Hear me when I tell you, there is no such thing as ghosts. They do not exist. They will never belong in that book my father left you. All right? You will never find one."

"You said we can feel lots of things that we cannot see," I point out.

She stares at me sadly. "Do you feel anyone here, Ramya?"

I stare back at her, and my eyes are suddenly tight and tense. I blink rapidly. When I speak, my voice is hoarse. "No."

She nods once. "Exactly."

Then she is back on her path, walking with a determination that forces me to hurry to keep up.

★

MARLEY AND I PRETEND TO be asleep when Aunt Leanna tucks us both in. It's only once we hear her reach the bottom of the tower stairs that we cast off our duvets and hurry to the window, pulling coats on over our pajamas and slipping on shoes.

"I definitely got a splinter last night," grumbles Marley as I lift the pane.

"Yeah, yeah, we'll put some witch hazel on it," I tell him. "For now, we've got things to find. You'll never guess what this man told me about by the loch today."

I tried to bring it up at dinner, but Opal pointed her finger at the radio, causing the music to drown me out.

The oak tree is back. Alona allows us to climb

onto her branches, only this time she doesn't wait for us to scale down. She decreases in size, shrinking until she is a small oak, the size of a child. Only once we hop onto the grass does she transform, back into her humanlike form.

"That is definitely impressive," I muse, unsure of what you say when your new acquaintance can change into a tree and back.

"Thanks," she says breezily. "Follow me."

She saunters away, forcing Marley and me to bolt after her. Marley is trying to catch my eye. I know he's nervous about this new arrangement.

"Where are you taking us?" he asks, a little accusingly.

"You want to see more Hidden Folk for that book?" she calls back to him. "Then you need to go to the hidden places!"

I catch up to her, dragging Marley along with me. "Cool!"

"Hidden places?" Marley objects, pointedly looking around at the vast loch, the barren woods, and the long and lonely road. "Nothing is hidden around here!"

"You're not very imaginative, are you?" Alona replies chirpily.

"He's Gifted and Talented," I tell her, using air quotes and drawing out the second word for as long as my breath allows. I grin at Marley, who pretends to chase me for a few seconds. "He's logic and good grades and a teacher's pet. Plays the bagpipes—worst musical instrument to ever exist. So no. Not very imaginative."

"I've told you to stop being rude about the bagpipes."

"The day I stop being rude about your bagpipes is the day they lower me into the ground."

I laugh, but it dies quite quickly. School, fun, and musical instruments all seem like a million years ago now.

Marley perseveres. "But seriously, where are you taking us?"

We seem to be heading deeper into the woods, but they aren't too dense. We can still see both the loch on the left and the road on the right. The long sliver of water is always in our sights as we move into the night.

"Here!" Alona finally declares triumphantly.

I can see, secreted beneath fallen branches and a lot of foliage, a crumbling stone well. An ancient thing that must have been here for centuries. I approach it slowly, noting how dry it appears.

"What is it?"

Marley speaks from behind my left shoulder. His voice is resigned, a quiet and stoic tone that always alerts me to the presence of Glamour. I can tell, by that tone alone, that Marley cannot see the well. It has been Glamoured with magic, hiding it from humans.

Most humans. Not a witch who has the Sight, like me.

"It's an old well," I explain softly. I lean over and peer down into its seemingly bottomless entrance. "It's dry, but I can't see how far it goes."

"Pretty deep," Alona says, hoisting herself onto the stony edge of the well. "So, you coming?"

"As if!" snaps Marley, his directness making me start. "You've led me into some weird places, Ramya, but I'm not jumping into a potentially mile-deep well that I cannot see!"

Alona smiles sweetly at him. "You stay here, then."

I frown at her. "Not going to happen. Where I go, he goes."

"And vice versa," Marley adds.

Alona is puzzled for a moment, glancing between the two of us. Then her face softens sheepishly, and she nods. "Well, it's not too bad a fall. It shouldn't hurt."

"The word 'shouldn't' is doing a lot of heavy lifting there," I say.

I turn to tell Marley that I'll go first, but I stop. He looks different. Strange. He's staring at the ground and is unimaginably still.

"You all right?" I ask.

He is breathing deeply and still staring at the ground. We stand in silence for a good while before he finally nods. "Fine."

I don't really believe him, but I don't want to push.

Not at this moment with a mysterious well behind us both.

I mount the thing, swinging my legs over the opening. "Marley. If this breaks my ankles, I'll scream. Then you smack her for leading us here."

Alona snorts, and Marley smiles reluctantly. I take a deep breath. I have had a few sprained ankles in my thirteen years. As a dyspraxic, I fall pretty often. Injuries are part of the package.

"If you can't do it unafraid, just do it afraid," I mutter, closing my eyes.

I let go and drop.

CHAPTER SEVEN

FAIRY TALE

The drop is long, and it makes my stomach shoot up inside my body. I flinch and clench and, without even meaning to do it, I'm hovering. My whole body is suspended midfall, and the shock of it causes my eyes to pop open.

My power slips in when I need it to. When I don't even mean to use it.

The sudden awareness causes my muscles to relax, and before I can celebrate for another millisecond, I'm falling again.

I don't hit hard ground, however; I hit some sort of net. I puff out a relieved breath and call up to Marley.

"It's safe, Marley! Alona, help him climb in!"

I can hear them preparing for his turn from

above, while I roll away from the net and onto the ground. I expect it to be muddy and marshy, but it's cold stone. I open my palm to create a kind of spark, and it briefly illuminates the underground tunnel I have found myself in. It stretches far ahead of me, ending in darkness once more. Whatever lies ahead is a mystery.

I startle as Marley's body suddenly slams into the net beside me. Alona follows, gracefully transforming into a leaf before she hits the netting. She humanizes once she's safe and beams at the two of us. I haul Marley to his feet, smiling grimly at his horrified expression.

"Lucky this net is here," I say, slapping his shoulder.

"Oh, it's not a net—it's an old stoor worm nest," says Alona.

Marley is horribly green, which halts my curiosity about what kind of a creature that is. "Okay. That's . . . great. So great. Are we going this way?"

I stare down the long tunnel, still nurturing the spark in my palm.

"Yes!" Alona says delightedly.

We set off. I can feel water even though I can't see any. The underground tunnel, which may in fact be a catacomb for extinct creatures, is eerily quiet. I can hear Marley's anxious breathing, but Alona is almost dancing, she is so relaxed.

"Where exactly are we going?" I ask.

She doesn't answer. Instead, she signals for us to turn left, just up ahead. When we do, it leads us to a door shaped like a hexagon. I'm reminded of the very first time I went down to the real Grassmarket, hidden underneath Edinburgh.

Alona knocks a particular kind of knock, and a small slot in the door slides open. Marley and I have to stifle gasps as three eyes stare out of the tiny space.

"Dryad?"

"Here to see Fog."

The three eyes disappear, and the strangely shaped door opens like a great vault, letting us inside. I stare up at the three-eyed troll and then quickly turn away.

Hidden Folk hate being stared at, just like any other person.

The room we have entered is enough of a distraction. It's an enormous hall with pillars and nooks on the side. In the center is a massive pool. A bath, with hot steam rising from it. The water is the color of marble, and there are all kinds of Hidden Folk swimming happily inside it.

"Most Hidden Folk in these parts are water creatures," Alona tells us conversationally. "So they like to relax here."

I'm wary of seeing that ceasg in the large bathing pool, but it seems to be full of Blue Men and a few

Hulders. They relax in the heat, their tails splashing about happily.

"This is weird, even for Hidden Folk," Marley says wearily, following me as I track Alona through the great hall.

As we make our way through the crowds gathered around the large bath, a hand reaches out from one of the nooks and grabs my elbow.

"Fancy a palm reading?"

"No, thanks, I'm good . . ." The words die on my lips as I lay eyes upon a very elderly woman who appears to be carrying her own head.

"Oh my G—"

"Hulder." Alona suddenly reappears, gently steering me away from the jarring sight. "Once they're a few centuries old, their heads fall off and they have to carry them. You'll get used to it."

"No," Marley and I both say in chorus. "We won't."

Alona leads us down to the back of the hall, where a little nook houses a man in green robes. He seems to be in some sort of trance. He is about my dad's age, and he seems entirely human.

"Fog!" Alona slips into the space next to him. There is a little stone table in front of them, with seating all around it. I can tell by Alona's tone of voice that this is someone she respects and cares about.

I slide into one of the seats across from the two of them, and Marley joins me quickly.

"These are my new friends," Alona says, and she places extra meaning in the word "friends," trying it out on her tongue, tasting it, as if she has never been able to say it before. "Ramya and Marley."

I can't remember if we ever actually told Alona our names, but then again, she has been listening to all of us outside the house for some time. I'm reminded of the fact that she was able to find the house, which must mean that she does not wish any harm to us.

I can't really imagine Alona wishing harm to anyone. She has the nature of a Labrador.

"This is Fog," she tells us. "He made me."

"Right," I say slowly, glancing sideways at Marley, who is every bit as bemused as I am. "What does that mean exactly?"

Fog's eyes are still closed, and he doesn't seem to hear us. Alona seems unbothered as she answers, "He's a Druid. They're the ones that can make dryads. I'm the first he's made in years."

I slip my grandfather's book and my pen out of the tote bag on my shoulder, flipping it open to a new page.

I write *DRUID* in large letters at the top of the page and start scribbling what Alona has just said.

Marley blinks. "So you're just a normal tree until some . . ."

"Druid," Alona supplies.

"Thank you. Until some Druid comes along and zaps you?"

Fog's eyes finally open, and they settle upon Marley unflinchingly. "It is a little more complex than 'zapping,' young man."

"You're a kind of magician," I say encouragingly.

"That's not a word any of us recognize," he says curtly. "I'm a Druid. We access magic in specific forms. We are leaders within the community. I do not pull rabbits out of a hat or saw people in half for money."

Marley gulps, but I merely narrow my eyes. I don't do very well with authority (at least, that was the general theme of my school reports). This Druid certainly thinks highly of himself, with his robes and his solitary meditation. Good for him, but I'm impressive too. I doubt he can fly. I doubt he can command water.

Just because that's on hiatus for me at the moment, it doesn't make it any less impressive.

"What's in it for the Druid?" I ask. "If you create a dryad, what's in for you?"

He fixes me with a cold stare. "Loyalty."

His answer is unsettling. There are plenty of untold stories behind it, hinting at a bond that is more complex than it may seem. I have a thousand questions, and my pen is poised to make notes when a hair-raising scream causes all my attention to shift.

Fog instantly pulls the curtains of the nook tightly closed, leaving only the smallest gap for us to see through. The entire hall has fallen silent, and the Hidden Folk who were happily soaking in the large bath have all frozen still.

I squint through the narrow slit of the curtain, and my pulse quickens as I see the cause of the scream.

Fae.

Just one of them. One with icy hair and bright white circles in his eyes. He is holding a very small and young troll by her hair. Her tail is swishing back and forth in agitation, and her stubby feet are kicking at the nothingness of the air as she is held above the stonework of the room.

"I'm just here," the faerie says, in a voice full of both poise and poison, "to ask a few questions. I'm looking for a very specific creature, rumored to be hidden in these parts. If I like your answers, or you tell me where it is, I'll let this one live."

"Fae," I whisper to Marley. He closes his eyes, and Alona makes a small squeak of fear. Fog whispers something to her, and she nods before transforming into a leaf. He carefully puts her into the pocket of his jacket. I turn back to the gap in the curtain, hungry to see what the faerie will do.

"This is not how we handle things," a voice says.

Hidden Folk, and the faerie, turn to look at a Hulder. She appears to be about Opal's age, and she stands bravely in the middle of the pool, glaring up at the faerie. "Put her down."

The faerie's expression does not change. He can sense all the fear in the room, and the energy of it must be enough to fuel him, like food. He doesn't put the little troll down; instead, he gives her a violent shake.

She starts to cry.

I'm already beginning to move, without even realizing it, when Marley grabs my shoulder.

"Don't," he hisses. "That's what he wants. They want to know where you are."

"I'm here," I snap back, quietly but fiercely. "They know we're in Loch Ness. Portia phoned the house. They can't find us there. We're safe when we're home; they can't find it."

"Let's be safe here, too," Marley fires back desperately.

"Sorry, Marley," I say sharply. "Can't just sit here."

I wrench the curtain open and pull it tightly closed behind me as I step out into the lights of the large hall. I can get myself into trouble, but they don't need to be dragged into it. I step forward to the edge of the pool and feel a thrum of triumph as the water reacts to my presence. It twitches and hums, enough for everyone in and around it to notice.

I walk on it. The water hardening beneath each step, solidifying. I face the faerie square on, standing upon the water as if it were just a wet woodland path.

Gasps and murmurs ripple through the room.

"Put the baby down," I tell the faerie, my voice colder and angrier than it was when this all began. When I was just a dyspraxic kid who hated school and didn't like looking too closely at people. "Gently. Or I'll make you."

The room is silent. A horrified, frightened kind of silence.

I can see confusion and curiosity enter the piercing eyes of the faerie. Callous cruelty and chaos take a step to the side for a moment as the creature ponders me.

I've clearly surprised him.

"What are you?" he asks, and his voice makes me think of carrion crows.

"I'm a witch," I tell him, proud of the audible reaction these words cause.

He sneers. "A very small one."

I raise my hand with the speed of a whip, and water shoots out of the pool to drench the faerie, enough to shock him into dropping the little troll.

The Hulder is there in an instant to scoop her up, and she runs for the entrance without turning back.

We can all hear the cries echoing down the tunnel.

"Is that the best you can do?" snarls the faerie, his rage palpable enough to cause other Hidden Folk to start edging toward the only exit. "Splash people?"

"No," I say, my voice soft. I'm a stranger to myself in this moment, as if someone else is speaking for me. "I could probably drown you."

Something flickers across the faerie's face. He is not willing to call my bluff, and a part of me is disappointed.

"Whatever creature you're hunting for in these parts, it doesn't want to be found," a Blue Man says, his voice civil and composed. "There have been stories of a monster in the loch for centuries. But the stoor worm is long gone. Nothing remains there now but fish and Hidden Folk."

"Maybe I don't seek the made-up object of human idiocy," the faerie says, causing me to roll my eyes.

"Why are you lot always so pretentious?" I mock. "There is no Loch Ness Monster. You can't come in here, trying to torture people into telling you about something that isn't real. Give me a fiver, I'll go to the tourist shop and buy you one of those plushies. The monster is not real!"

"It is real."

Everyone turns to the source of the words.

It's a woman with silvery skin and large, sad eyes.

I know she isn't human, and yet there is nothing specifically mythical about her appearance. She just radiates difference.

"Selkie," the Blue Man says, speaking slowly and gently, as if afraid of hurting her feelings. "Your kind are long gone from the loch, and so is any—"

"I've seen it," the selkie continues. "But I've seen something even stranger. Something with no name. Something that moves like a riddle."

I notice how hungry the faerie now seems. Clearly, this information is valuable to him. The selkie's gaze is faraway, as if she is remembering something troubling.

She seems haunted.

"It's not human, not Hidden, either."

Her words remind me of the Stranger. Though I can't conjure up his face, the feelings that he leaves behind are in my memory. His magic is so far beyond that of any normal Hidden creature. He can disappear and reappear at will.

Plus, something more. Something frightening.

"Where did you see it?" asks the faerie. He is clearly trying to be gentle, but it's something he's not capable of conveying.

"If I tell you"—the selkie speaks in a voice that

makes everyone around her take a small step away, as if her sad voice is repellent to them—"will you destroy it?"

The faerie hesitates, and I smirk. Unlike sirens, the fae cannot lie. They must dance around the truth instead.

"We need to find it," he finally settles on.

"Who is 'we'?" I demand.

The faerie hisses.

"The fae are working with sirens!" I shout, letting my voice echo against the walls so that everyone can hear. The statement causes people to hum and whisper nervously.

"Sirens," the selkie says venomously. She turns to the faerie. "Is that true?"

The faerie takes too long to think of a way to answer, as he's unable to lie and say no. His pause is noticeable, and the Hidden Folk cry out with accusatory voices.

"Let the little witch drown him!" someone yells from the back.

I'm startled. They are completely serious. I watch as fear flickers in the face of the faerie, and I feel something unpleasant knot inside me.

"You're hunting this mystery creature for the sirens," I say, staring down the white-eyed creature. "Why?"

Smugness sparks in the faerie's face. "Because when we give it to her, she will win."

She. Portia. I don't need him to say her name.

"She's not going to win," I say flatly. "Ever. I know what she's trying to do. She's trying to divide us. Create chaos. But she's not going to win."

The faerie's eyes continue to glint. "Oh, it's so much more than that," he says, too gently. Too quietly. "She's reordering this world. Mending it."

My voice cowers inside my throat. *Reordering.*

The word is distressing.

"If you see the creature," the faerie says slowly, addressing the entire room, "it would be in your best interests to tell us."

"This loch and its Hidden Folk are protected," I snap. "By me and some other witches who don't have time for this nonsense. You can take your threats and move out."

The faerie considers me, clearly wondering how much power I actually wield. However, the grim faces of the Hidden Folk and the angry energy of the selkie cause him to steadily back down. He moves toward the exit of the large hall, casting one final glance over his shoulder.

"I'll give Portia your regards, little witch."

"Sure," I say. "Then give her this."

I throw him my rudest hand gesture, one that

would make Mum smack my leg if she were here. Which she is not.

Only once the faerie is gone and I am back on dry land do I feel Fog, Alona, and Marley at my side.

"What do we do?" asks Marley, his voice shaken.

"Easy," I reply. "We find that creature before they do."

CHAPTER EIGHT

HOAX

It's morning once again, and Marley and I are exhausted all over. We can barely lift our spoons for our cereal, and I spill the milk twice. The only thing giving me even a fraction of energy is the knowledge that we're going on another quest. We are going to find that creature before Portia's army does.

Leanna is marking some of Marley's homework. She's been lying to the school about both of us coming down with terrible chicken pox. We only have a week left of term, so the teachers don't seem to be fighting her too much. They know Marley is smart enough to teach himself at this point, and they're probably pretty relieved to be free of me.

"I'm starting to believe you *are* both ill," Leanna says. "What's wrong?"

"The wind is loud in that tower," I say, not untruthfully. "It's hard to get a good night's sleep."

"Oh," she says, frowning in concern. "Well, maybe we can move you both."

"It's fine, Mum," says Marley, throwing me a glance and shaking his head just slightly. "We're all right."

"Well, okay." She stares over at the windowsill. "You know . . . I really hate winter."

She waves her hand softly. Some dying plants outside start to bloom again. Only a little, but it is beautiful magic. She causes some bluebells to appear in front of us on the table.

"Blue is one of the rarest colors in nature, you know," she says, and she looks directly at me. "But things that are rare tend to be the best, don't they?"

I smile. Aunt Leanna's magic is softer and quieter than her sisters' but no less impressive or important.

"Where's Opal?" I ask, staring at her empty chair in the breakfast nook.

"She's working on an extremely taxing spell at the moment," Leanna says. "It's taking up a lot of her energy."

I narrow my eyes. "What kind of spell?"

"Nothing to concern yourself about."

Opal stands in the doorway, and, although she

spoke the words with her usual dryness, she sounds absolutely exhausted. She's wearing a ratty oversized knitted sweater with matching black shorts. Her legs are long and thin, and she seems so young this morning. Dark circles and her hair scraped into a messy updo.

Opal is neurodivergent like me. She gets overwhelmed. She processes things at her own pace. She likes routine. Her hands sometimes shake, she gets headaches easily, and she is blunt and direct and to the point. She's also loyal. Brave. The only person who came to that island to save me when I thought I was completely alone in the world.

"Come on, you," she says to me. "Marley has English homework, and you've got witchcraft theory. Let's go."

I leap to my feet and cackle in Marley's face. "Enjoy your boring book about a whale."

"Yeah, yeah," he mumbles.

I follow Opal up to the first floor, to the small library.

I've poked my head in a couple of times, but we've never taken lessons in here.

"Are we going to practice launching books at people?" I ask gleefully.

"We're doing theory today," she says, gesturing for me to sit at a small table by the window, where the sun is pouring in. "Not practice."

I groan. "Theory of what?"

She sits at the table herself, not speaking until I sulkily collapse into the chair across from her.

"Curses."

My mouth drops open and I make a noise of elation. "No!"

"Yes!"

"I get to learn how to curse people."

"No," she says, frowning at me. "I'm teaching you about them. Why would you want to curse someone?"

I shrug. "There are some kids in my old class who could do with a curse. That baroness who came to our school, the one who was secretly a siren. Portia."

"Ramya," she says carefully, "you need to know about all kinds of witchcraft. But magic is not your weapon. It's your defense. It's a gift. Not something to use to hurt people."

I exhale. "Fine. Tell me about a hypothetical curse I'll never be allowed to cast."

She smirks. "Remember, magic is different with every single person. No two spells are the same. One witch cannot imitate another."

"When you cast that medusa hex on Ren," I butt in, "when you turned him to stone, was that a curse?"

"No," she says, and a mournful look comes over

her face for a moment. "That was exactly that. A hex. A curse . . . a curse is irreversible. It cannot be undone."

"Not even by the witch who casts it?"

She shakes her head. "I've never heard of a curse being reversed. By anyone."

"Have you ever cast one?"

"No."

"Have you ever wanted to?"

Something flashes across her face. She censors it quickly, before I can name the emotion. She peers out the window and then looks back at me. "Yes."

I appreciate the honest response. It sits between the two of us for a moment.

"Who was it?" I ask.

At first, I think she won't answer. Then, "Someone I used to know."

"A friend?"

"Once."

"You're not friends anymore?"

Her eyes shine in the crisp winter sun coming in from the window, while her lips attempt a smile. "No."

"I'm not sure they'll want to be friends again if you curse them, Aunt Opal."

She laughs, and then her face contorts for a split second. She laughs again, uneasily, and looks quickly away. She blinks a couple of times. "No, probably not."

"What did they do?"

She sniffs once and starts sorting through a pile of books that were already on the table. "Oh . . . lots of things."

"Maybe you can make up?"

She touches the corner of her eye with the pad of her forefinger. "You know, Dad—your grandpa—he used to always say something. 'The one thing evil cannot endure, the one thing it cannot bear, is your forgiveness.' "

I wrinkle my nose. "What? That doesn't make any sense. Forgiving people means letting them off the hook. Why would that—"

"Like I said, it was just something he would say," Opal remarks swiftly. She seems to have shaken herself back into teaching mode. "Now come on. You've got to read these and note down the similar points in each text."

I flip open the first dusty book with a grimace.

"And I'll give you a tip," she adds. "Casting a curse, or any spell, should never come from a place of anger or hatred."

I glance up at her. She is watching me with a knowing stare. I suddenly think of the faerie.

"Noted," I say quietly.

I begin to read.

*

I'M STILL THINKING ABOUT CURSES and Aunt Opal when Alona appears by our window at nine o'clock that night. Marley eagerly climbs out and onto the branches. I lift my tote bag with Grandpa's book, feeling just a little less enthusiastic than usual.

"Come on," Marley says impatiently. "New quest, you said."

I smile and climb out carefully. "Yeah. Back into the fray."

I can't help but feel like we should be back in Edinburgh. Freddy's emails have been sporadic and a little clipped, as if he doesn't have as much time to write. He says things are different there now, and not in a good way.

They need help. I can tell.

I just don't know how to get to them. I could never fly to Edinburgh by myself, let alone with Marley on my back. Even Opal couldn't fly that far.

At least, I don't think she could.

We hit the grass and make our way toward the winding loch. I told Alona to ask all the Hidden Folk she knew, including her maker the Druid, about the mysterious creature.

"That selkie has agreed to speak with us," she announces as we scamper down to the bank.

As we reach it, I do what has always been

instinctual to me. I kneel and touch the water. I channel the pulses of magic inside me into my hands and press them against the cold, ancient loch.

It occurs to me that this mass of water has been around for longer than anyone I know, or have ever known, and it will still be here after I am gone.

The electricity I feel in my hand moves into the loch. Ripples start to swell across the glassy water. I move back a little, ordering Alona and Marley to do the same. We don't need the ceasg to return.

She does not. Another creature appears where she once did.

The selkie. She moves like a seal through the cold waves and breaks the surface in front of the three of us.

"Haven't been in these waters for the longest time," she says, shaking off drops of liquid. She sounds contemplative.

"Why?" Marley asks, taking in the majesty of another creature who does not feel the need to Glamour.

"My family were chased out a long time ago," she says quietly. "I moved to the sea. But I come back in the winter months. To remember."

"Who chased them out?" I ask defensively. "Sirens? Fae?"

She looks straight at me. "No. Humans."

I shrink back a little. "Oh."

"Can you tell us more about this creature you saw?" Marley asks her.

She shivers. "It's not what the humans think. It could be a different monster entirely. It is not some underwater creature, or some dinosaur of the deep. It's . . . like a ghost."

I think of Angus and his stories of the villagers and the Hidden Folk who swore they had seen a spirit from beyond the grave. "What makes you say that?"

The selkie glances around furtively. "It knew things about me. Wordless things. I only saw it from a distance; at first I thought I must be hallucinating. It can shift and transform. It is . . . quite horrifying."

I share a glance with Marley and Alona. They are as baffled as I feel.

"I can't tell you how it can exist," the selkie adds. "I've never seen anything like it. It has the stature and size of a human, but there is something so unnatural about it. It's . . . it feels cruel. It does not speak. But it knows things."

"What do you mean, what things?" I ask the question a little frantically, as the selkie is already starting to move back into deeper water.

"Things I don't want to remember," she whispers before her lips disappear beneath the breaking waves.

I make a noise of frustration, and for a moment

I consider diving in after her. I obviously don't. I might have a special relationship with water, my magic may call to it, but I cannot stand the icy temperature of the loch.

Instead, I dash out onto it. The way I did upon the River Forth, now so long ago. I dance across the flat surface of the loch, connecting with the water so it holds me up. Alona watches in astonishment, her eyes wide at the sight of my true nature. I don't Glamour the way some Hidden Folk choose to, but I mask. I hide my potential. I dial it down.

I bound across the water and eventually stand still about ten meters from the shore.

"Stop showing off and get back on land now," Marley calls out.

"I'm good," I call back, needing the mask to be gone right now. "It's fine."

"That mermaid thing might come back," he insists. "Come on."

"Not scared of anything in this loch," I retort. I start to dance again, moving like an ice skater across the unfrozen water. I dart and leap and command the fluid glass.

I have a lot of feelings. I have feelings about fae and sirens stalking innocent Hidden Folk. I have feelings about the ghost that has allegedly been seen around these parts. I have feelings about Aunt Opal and her stoic secrets. I have feelings about Alona, our new friend, with her giddy freedom and lack of worries. I have feelings about Freddy, my old friend, who is far away and distant over emails. I have feelings about the absolute idiocy of forgiving enemies. I have feelings about Grandpa not being here to see me dance on the water. I have feelings about Mum and Gran disappearing without saying goodbye, without even explaining why or where, without giving me any assurance about it, without saying why it was so important—so important that I cannot know the reason, wasn't worth a conversation, wasn't worth—

I lose concentration and fall into the icy depths. I drop like a stone.

I open my mouth automatically to cry out, and water rushes in. I push up, using every muscle to get to the top. It is too heavy underwater to use the full force of my magic. I am about to breach the surface when I feel something awe-inspiring and terrifying. Something is underneath me, something large, and it pushes me up. It forces me out of the water. It gives me enough of a launch to fly over to the shore.

"What happened?" yelps Marley while Alona rubs my arms feverishly. She doesn't need to; the shock and adrenaline are distracting me from the awful cold.

I stare out at the water.

"I don't know," I gabble, all bravado gone. "I have no idea."

I scramble forward, now pressing both hands to the water. I once summoned the kelpies of Edinburgh this way. The action called them to us, despite how reticent and reluctant they were around humans.

I try now. Letting the water sing.

Something breaches. Something large, right at the spot in Loch Ness where I dropped. It swims closer, standing to its full height when the water is shallow enough.

"Oh my G—" Marley croaks out the words and then falls silent, completely petrified.

"It's true," Alona gasps, more still than I have ever seen her. "Those silly human stories, they were all true."

"Not exactly," I murmur, taking in the enormous creature. It's the size of an elephant. It's scaly and rough and has four legs and a long slender tail. It has a colossal pair of wings. It is blue. A deep, electric blue. Its face has been drawn in fairy stories for as long as I can remember, with flared nostrils and large teeth, yet seeing it in person is more astonishing than I could ever have imagined.

"It's not a monster," I finally breathe. "It's a dragon."

CHAPTER NINE

WHEN MAGIC IS BLUE

Marley grabs my hand, and Alona presses against my other side. The three of us cower in front of this intimidating creature as it blocks out the moon and stars before us. The shallows of Loch Ness only reach the creature's knees, causing me to wonder what its feet are like.

"Should we run?" asks Marley, his hand squeezing tightly to mine. Alona is trembling, but she remains in her human form, defiant despite the obvious fear she is feeling. "What if it breathes fire, in stories they always breathe fire."

I keep staring up at the dragon. It has deep blue eyes that match its scales and body.

"I wouldn't trust those stories," I tell Marley,

keeping my eyes glued to the blue reptile. "They say a lot of things that aren't true."

I take a step forward, letting go of Marley's hand and extracting myself from Alona's grip. They both make noises of protest, but I ignore them. The dragon makes a chuffing sound. A grunt. Yet no fire comes out of its nostrils, only air.

I wade into the water, still too pumped with adrenaline to feel the full sharpness of the icy cold. I reach out a hand to touch its snout. The dragon intuitively flinches away, even gurgling slightly in objection. I still my hand, deciding not to press any closer unless welcomed.

"It pushed me out of the water," I tell the others. "It came up from the deep."

"I think," Alona says slowly, "it's a she."

"This is Nessie," Marley says dazedly, taking a minuscule step forward too. "We're actually looking at Nessie."

The dragon chuffs once more, at the mention of that name, as if rejecting it. It causes Marley to step back again. I admire her giant wings, noticing that they're not only blue, but transparent. Almost fragile. The dragon folds them in and roars, moving back out toward the deeper section of the loch.

"Wait," I call, pushing against the water and following her. "Do you Glamour?"

"I don't think the possibly fire-breathing dragon speaks English!" Marley rasps.

As if to spite and defy him, the dragon sinks down into the water. I can see the blue scales beneath, but Marley gasps, leaping forward.

"It's gone!" he cries.

"You can't see her?" I demand, laughing shrilly at the realization.

The dragon can Glamour. She can disguise herself, blend into her surroundings like a water chameleon. That is why no film crew has ever discovered her. The tourists who've come, desperate to explore and unmask the monster, have probably sailed their boats right by the dragon, never knowing what was underneath because her Glamour perfectly hid her.

The dragon resurfaces calmly. I fully believe I can see a glint of satisfaction in her eye.

"The few people who spotted you must have been like me," I say softly. "That's why no one really believes them."

The dragon doesn't react. I step closer again, holding up my hands to try to communicate how badly I just want to connect. Peacefully.

"Careful," Marley says, though he sounds a little more assured.

I approach. "I think you're magnificent."

The dragon chuffs once more, though this time it's a little fainter.

"I'm Ramya, a witch; this is Alona, a dryad; and that's my cousin, Marley. A Capricorn."

"Thanks," Marley says dully. "But I'm a Sagittarius."

"We don't want to hurt you or hunt you or let anyone else see you," I say. "I swear. But we've never seen anything like you."

The dragon straightens her stature a little. I regard her great wings thoughtfully.

"You live in the water, but you can fly?"

Part reptile, part mammal, part bird? She doesn't appear to have gills, so she must hold her breath while under the water. I wonder if the wings are just for display.

As if reading my mind, the dragon stretches her wings, and they cast off droplets of water, soaking the three of us. I laugh, thrilled.

"You *can* fly," I say to myself, completely enraptured.

The dragon bows her head and lays the wing nearest us down, almost like a smooth, watery set of stairs. I know at once what the huge creature is challenging me to do, and it sets every fiber of my body on fire with excitement.

I continue forward.

"No, Ramya," groans Marley. "Don't do something stupid."

"You know me," I say to him, my eyes locked on the dragon's gaze. "Stupid is someone else's clever."

I carefully climb onto the dragon's back as gently as I can. I shuffle forward once I'm astride her torso to sit up front, where the neck meets the body. There are sharp horns peppered across the scales, and I use them as handles, gripping on tight.

"Right, you've had a sit," Marley says, sounding like Mum. "Time to come down."

Alona bursts out laughing and transforms into a green vine. She tenderly curls around the dragon's blue neck, turning herself into a set of reins. I bark out a laugh of my own and turn to Marley. "You coming?"

"Absolutely not," he says, snorting in disbelief. "Don't you dare do it. I'm not explaining to the aunts that you got killed trying to fly a dragon."

"Marley," I say calmly, smiling an indulgent smile. "We are not going to die. If we fall off, I will not let you drop. We'll be fine."

He does not seem reassured in any way. He eyes the dragon with complete distrust.

"Marley!" I cry, laughing giddily. "How many people get to say that they have even seen the Loch Ness . . . Dragon? Let alone ridden her. Get. On."

He gives it another moment of thought, and I can see the two sides of his brain warring over it. The sensible, logical side of him doesn't want the other, quieter part to have any fun or joy. It worries and needles and is constantly afraid for him. It silences the whispers in his head that tell him it is okay to enjoy something, without dress-rehearsing all the ways it can go wrong.

He shakes his head.

I don't push. I do not tell him he's being ridiculous or weird or silly. Maybe I would have a year ago. Now I'm certain Marley is sort of the bravest person I know. He's not telling me he thinks this will be too dangerous because he's scared.

More because he can see multiple endings. To every story, to every task. Marley can see every eventuality, like a clairvoyant.

He doesn't want to risk things that are important.

I like risk, though. I'm not like Marley. In fact, if I'm honest, it's the reason there was friction between us when we first met. He is Gifted and Talented—the boy who teachers drag out of history when there's a school visitor. They like to parade him around as the perfect example, the child and student we should all aspire to be.

It wasn't good for people like me, and it wasn't always good for Marley. Yes, praise must be nice

(I wouldn't really know), but after so much of it, I don't know if Marley knows who he is without it.

Mum sometimes says, "Why can't you be more like your cousin?"

Because I'm neurodivergent. No molding, no occupational therapy, no tough love or extra help or special education is going to change that. I'm never going to be a neurotypical child.

I was meant to be so much more. That's why I'm not afraid. Maybe neurotypical children were made for behavior charts and school reports and following commands, but I'm not. I feel out of place in a classroom. I feel wrongly made whenever I'm stood up next to my peers at Field Day or Open House Day.

But I feel very at home on this dragon.

"I'll be safe, Marley," I tell him frankly, and as I say the words, I can feel the dragon start to tense and move, getting ready for flight. Her shoulders shift, her flank twitches, and her feet pull up a little from beneath the water.

I let out a yell as the creature suddenly hurtles into a run, using the vast openness of the loch as a path for launch, spreading her great wings apart like a sail about to catch the wind. I grip on with everything that I have, and the air in my lungs is squashed by the air I choke on as the dragon gains incredible speed.

I know and feel exactly when we are about to

take flight. It is a feeling without description, that I now know in my own body. A plane about to lift its wheels off the runway causes a certain faintness in your legs and a hook in your stomach, but it's nothing compared to flying yourself.

Or flying upon a dragon.

The dragon ascends. I hold on even more tightly. She lifts her feet up into her body and commands her wings with the strength of multiple men rowing a ship. I cannot contain my yell of delight and terror as the dragon flies. She shoots up into the sky with more speed and agility than I could ever have imagined. I always thought dragons would fly like eagles. This dragon flies like a swift.

The scream in my throat turns into a shout of triumph and elation as we dive and soar through the skies above the loch. When the dragon slows down to a gentle speed over the surface of the water, I take a moment to admire the blue scales.

A stunning blue.

The dragon, as if hearing me, lets out a snort of air and climbs higher once more. I instinctively let go. I swan-dive, letting gravity haul me closer to the water. Right as I'm about to hit the cold loch with my nose, I harness. I trust.

I fly. Just like the dragon. I cannot rise as quickly, I cannot soar as high, but I can fly.

I suddenly remember sitting on the bike sheds at

school, back in Edinburgh. I remember how nervous Mr. Ishmael was, scared I might fall and hurt myself even though I was only five feet above the ground.

If only he could see me now. Soaring with a dragon, a blue dragon, that legends have hinted at, yet most people cannot see. A dragon with myth and stories etched into her sapphire scales.

Later, I fill Grandpa's book with pages and pages on the dragon I call Blue in my head. It reminds me of being in the streets of Edinburgh with Marley, cataloguing the strange and wondrous people we met. It all feels so long ago now, and everything has suddenly become so serious and grown-up. The world seems less populated by adults, now just full of big, frightened children.

Yet a dragon. A dragon that not only feels impossible, but also hopeful. I write down everything I can about Blue, and I cannot quite believe that she is real.

I'm a dyspraxic witch with a bad temper and I'm soaring side by side with a blue dragon.

"Like Aunt Leanna said," I say to nobody. "Blue *is* rare in nature."

Right now, there is a little blue in me, too.

CHAPTER TEN

VISITORS

When Marley and I are back in our beds, I stare up at the ceiling for a good twenty minutes. I'm too wired to sleep, too tired to speak. Marley is sitting up against the wall on his side of the tower bedroom. He is staring into nothingness. I finally sit up myself, putting the idea of sleep to one side for a moment, and we lock eyes.

"Marley," I choke out, almost hysterical with tiredness and the tingling feeling that you get after doing something life-changing. "A *d*—"

"Dragon!" he spits out before I can, his eyes wide and his voice higher than I have ever heard it. "That is, hands down, the maddest, scariest, most awe-some thing I've ever seen during this weird quest."

"A dragon!"

"A dragon!"

"Like, not even a little one," I gasp, hugging my pillow to my stomach and rocking back and forth. "A massive, scary BLUE DRAGON."

We laugh, trying to smother the sound so we don't wake the aunts.

"I wish . . . ," Marley says, and his excitement suddenly fades. He looks down. I frown, glancing over at him in confusion.

"What is it?" I ask.

His face crumples, and he doubles over for a moment. When he sits up straight once more, I can see silvery streaks on his flushed face.

"Marley?" I say softly. "You okay?"

He sits quietly for a moment, making me wonder if he heard me. Then he speaks. "I just wish he were here. I wish he could have seen it."

Grandpa. Marley knew him more than I ever did.

They were close.

"I know."

Marley was quiet when the dragon finally landed on the edge of the water. We watched her disappear down into the loch, and we walked home in silence. I thought he was subdued out of shock, because of the unutterable feelings the dragon left behind.

Now I can see he's in the past.

"Ramya," he finally says, and there is a change in the room. Something in his voice is older, more serious, and totally new compared to the way that Marley normally speaks.

"Yes?"

"I saw him."

I blink. "What?"

"I saw him. I was watching you and the dragon, and then I saw something flash across the water. Then he was there. On the bank, a few yards away. I saw him."

I stare. "I don't—"

"Grandpa. I saw him."

At my old school in London, there was this staircase. It was steeper than the others. I used to pretend to lose my footing at the very top, only to grab onto my friend Sara. We would scream, she would chastise me, and I would laugh until my ribs hurt. Then, one day, she stepped away so I couldn't grab onto her. I almost fell. The fear and sense of betrayal were intense. It was a moment where the selfish part of me was forced to realize that this other person was just that. A person with real feelings and emotions.

This feels like that.

"Marley," I say. The conversation feels like broken glass. "That's not possible."

Something hardens in his face. "Yes, it is. Because that's what I saw. It was him."

"Marley—"

"No, don't do that. I nod and say 'okay' when

you say you can see water horses or women with tails or vampires in the library. Now *you* have to believe *me*."

"Ghosts aren't real. Aunt Opal said so."

"I saw him!"

I flinch. Marley never shouts.

"Okay. Fine. You saw him. What was he doing?"

"Just staring at me. I wanted to go over, but I couldn't move. Then he vanished."

"Into thin air?"

"Yes, when the dragon landed. But it was him. Absolutely him."

"Okay," I say stiffly, eyeing my cousin with a contained expression. "So we tell Aunt Opal."

I expect him to waver, to be unsure. Instead, he nods. "Fine."

I can't believe what I'm hearing. "You really saw him?"

"Yes!" he cries indignantly. "Why? Are you upset that I can finally see something you maybe can't?"

I glower at him. "Don't be like that."

"I'll tell Opal tomorrow. At dinner."

"Fine."

We sit in silence, staring at each other. There is a stiff, unfriendly feeling in the room with us now. He falls asleep before I do. I can still feel the soaring in my stomach, from the dragon ride, but it's tempered with anxiety about what Marley has told me.

Ghosts aren't real. I can see vampires, fae, trolls, and all other kinds of Hidden Folk. I am immune to sirens. But the one thing we both wanted when we began this quest, to see him again . . . we were told that would never be possible.

I refuse to let myself hope.

*

OPAL RESTS ALL DAY LONG.

When I ask Aunt Leanna why, she distracts me with treats and mumbles something about spell preparation and avoiding overstimulation.

We eat dinner in the dining room, and the phone rings as I'm about to bite into a piece of carrot. We all eye the landline, newly fixed by Opal. Leanna and Marley glance at me.

If it is a siren calling, only Opal and I are safe over the phone.

I lift the receiver, saying nothing as a greeting.

"It's polite to say 'hello' when you answer the phone."

Every muscle relaxes, and I roll my eyes. "Hi, Mum."

"Are you having dinner?"

"Yes."

"Are you eating everything Aunt Leanna has cooked for you?"

I glance toward the untouched broccoli and spinach on the side of my plate. "Yes."

"Liar."

I deliberately say nothing, using my silence as punishment. I can hear her sigh on the other end of the line.

"Where are you?" I finally ask, relenting slightly.

"London with Dad."

I feel a stab of relief, but I don't let it into my voice. "Where? The old house?"

"No. There's a coven I know, in Shoreditch. On Hoxton Street. You'd love it—their quarters are behind this little shopfront. Guess what they sell?"

I can tell she is trying to make up for disappearing in the night by being chatty. "Don't know."

A pause, but she perseveres. "Monster supplies."

I forget my huff for a moment to let out a noise of surprise. "Monster supplies?"

"Pretend ones. Cute little pieces of witch lore and 'dragon gold' for people. Really fun. It's like hiding in plain sight, you know?"

"Pretend dragon gold," I say musingly.

"Didn't have the heart to tell some tourists this morning that dragons have been gone for generations. But it's a cute little hiding place for now. And the coven is loyal to our side."

"Our side?"

"Whichever side Portia is not on. Speaking of which, can you put Aunt Opal on the phone, please?"

I am about to tell her that I can't, that her youngest sister is convalescing, when I suddenly feel a gentle hand move the phone from mine. Opal is beside me. She has ghosted into the room, and her creepily acute hearing seems to have alerted her. She gives me an assessing look as she puts the receiver to her ear.

"Yes, Cass?"

It's raining outside, and darkness has crept in.

Leanna steers me back to my seat and whispers that I only need to eat half the vegetables. I nod distractedly and glance over at Aunt Opal. She has her back to us, and her posture is straight and stiff.

She is listening and not speaking. Mum is obviously feeding her a ton of information that she's been gathering in London. I get to my feet and head for the door, mentally selecting which extension I'm going to listen in on. I slip across the hall and into the kitchen, taking every bit of care to lift the receiver of the telephone with as much gentleness as possible.

I usually have no control over my clumsiness, but when it comes to eavesdropping, I will force myself to be dexterous.

Mum is speaking when I put the phone to my ear. "—sort of like we expected. Anyway, Mike and I are hunkered down here, and it doesn't seem like

London has fallen. It's pretty much how it's always been."

"A den for sirens, then?" Opal speaks with bite in her words.

"Now, now," Mum says serenely.

"London is too stubborn to fall completely. Besides, they're too divided in the south."

The sirens? One thing I know about them is that they do not work well together.

"They're scattered and self-absorbed," Mum acknowledges. "It could be that Portia is using Edinburgh for a trial run."

"The spies have become very quiet," Opal says softly. "Whatever she's doing, it's having an effect."

I clap a hand over my mouth to stop myself from breathing too loudly, fearful of giving away my uninvited place in this conversation.

"So what is the long-term plan?" Mum says.

I nod unconsciously. I've been silently asking this question for days. We can't just hide out in our covens and quarters, waiting for the sirens and their lackeys to go away. Portia is not going away.

"I just need time," Opal finally says, and even though I know she's talking to her older sister, it feels as if she is speaking directly to me. "I need you to trust me. Give me time to prepare. No impulsive decisions, no attacks, no strikes. Just time. I'm handling this."

I gently put the phone down, not wanting to hear any more. I somehow know that nothing else is going to be said. I stare out of the kitchen window, into the garden. Alona is there. In her tree shape. She must feel me regarding her somehow, as she quickly transforms into her human self. She scurries to the window, which is slightly ajar.

I don't know why, but I feel like crying.

"Everything all right?" Alona asks.

She rests her chin upon her hands, laid gently on the windowsill, and she looks up at me with an expression that is older than the ones she usually gives us.

"Not really," I whisper hoarsely.

"Family troubles?"

I shrug. Then think for a moment. "You and the Druid?"

"Yes?"

"Is he like your father?"

"I suppose. Father, friend, god, mentor. Someone who brought me into the world. I suppose that makes him more of a mother than a father. Aren't they all those things?"

I swipe fiercely at my cheek. "Sometimes. Not mine, though."

"Where is she?"

"Not here. Never really here, if you know what I mean."

"I don't."

"I wasn't what she wanted," I say, laughing coldly. "She wanted a boy. I was supposed to be called Douglas. The room was blue and everything."

Sometimes I think about how Douglas was supposed to be. Probably really sporty and athletic. He wouldn't drop a million throws like me. Or fall down or trip over his own feet. He would do really well at school and the teachers would all love him. Pleasure to teach. Gifted and Talented. Named during assemblies. Kind of like Marley.

I cannot see Alona through the blur of tears, but I can feel her staring at me.

"Leanna loves Marley so much," I choke out, forcing a very unconvincing smile. "She watches him, even when it doesn't seem like she's doing it. She hugs him all the time. My mum never hugs me. She always looks at me like I'm an employee who's on their last warning."

Alona clears her throat and reaches out to touch my forearm. "I'm sorry. We all need light in order to grow."

"But you know what?" I feel a bitter taste in my mouth. "No matter how much Leanna loved Marley—and she does, more than anything—she still fell under a siren's spell. And at the end of everything, I was the one who stood alone on that island. Facing down a monster. Ready to save him."

I remember how alone I felt. How frightening it was. "I thought no one was coming for me. But I didn't care. I always thought I was a selfish person, and I sort of am. Sometimes. But it just had to be that way. They wanted Marley safe more than me. I was sure of it. So I just gave them what they wanted."

"Weren't you terrified?"

"Yes. But he's family. And my best friend. And when someone like that is in danger, you sort of forget about all the arguments and the sore feelings and bitter stuff. None of it matters anymore."

Doing the right thing becomes as easy as breathing when it's someone you love. I can't say it out loud because it's embarrassing and exposing. But that's how it feels.

"I'm just thinking about all of that tonight," I add, "because when the grown-ups are in bed, I'm going home."

Alona's green eyebrows shoot up into her hairline. "Home?"

"Yes. Edinburgh. I'm going back with the dragon.

"Tonight."

CHAPTER ELEVEN

GHOST TOWN

"It was here. Where I saw him."

Marley and I are by the bank of Loch Ness and I'm about to call Blue. Marley's mind is on other things, clearly.

"Marley," I say. "I believe you. I do. I just don't know if it's what it seems at first glance."

"Call this dragon," Marley replies stiffly. "I know what I saw."

I nod. "You don't have to come with me, you know."

"I want to."

"If flying makes you sick—"

"Ramya!"

"Okay, okay."

When the dragon appears, both of us forget the

quiet fight we were having. We stare up at the enormous beast with fear and awe.

"How are you going to tell it to get us to Edinburgh?" Marley murmurs.

It is a very fair question. "She understood me when I spoke to her last night."

"She?"

"I'm certain Alona was right."

"Next you'll be naming her."

I don't inform him that I already have.

The dragon stares at us coolly. I step toward her, with outstretched hands as usual. She watches me approach.

"Our friends back home may be in danger," I tell her, feeling foolish but willing to try. "In Edinburgh. The city, the capital. South. Could you fly us there? There's an island in the river; you can hide there while we search for them. It will be safe."

The dragon regards me with an expression that is not unlike the one Aunt Opal gives me when I'm impertinent.

Then she lowers her great wing. I release all the air I've been holding on to, and I mount up.

"Get up and hold on for dear life," I tell Marley.

"If I end up skydiving, tell the family it was all your fault."

"Get on."

Marley is tentative, cautious in the extreme as he

attempts to climb up onto the dragon. As he clambers on, Blue shifts sharply, causing Marley to squeak in terror as he almost slips off.

"Not funny," I mutter, and if dragons can laugh, this one does. Her shoulders move in a mischievous fashion.

Marley sits behind me, and I can feel how tense and unhappy he is.

"I'm not going to let you fall to your death, and we're not taking off until you acknowledge that," I tell him sternly.

As Marley grumbles and tries to settle, I spy Alona upon the bank of the loch. She looks more serious than I have ever seen her, causing my enthusiastic greeting to die on my lips.

"Be safe," she says softly.

"Come with us," I counter. "Come and see Edinburgh."

She tries to smile and fails. "It's all right. Not today. I can't Glamour well enough for a big city."

I want to laugh; Edinburgh is hardly a big city to me. Compared to London, it's a little hamlet. However, Alona only knows the nothingness and vast space of Loch Ness.

"Did you know, you can fit the whole human population in this water?" I tell her. "That's how big and deep it is. A city surely can't be as scary as that."

She shrugs and laughs a little darkly. "I'm scared

of all kinds of things. Better off here. Better off at home."

"Let's get this over with," Marley says from behind me.

"Okay," I say, nodding at Alona. "We'll see you when we're back."

"How do I know you'll come back?" she replies, and she looks as if she regrets saying it the moment it's out.

"Friends always come back."

We stare at each other, and she finally smiles, a genuine smile. I tap Blue gently and let out a cry of joy while Marley shouts, as we begin an immediate journey of flight, the dragon's wings beating against the water as she prepares to soar.

"Hang on!" I yell over the spray of water and pounding of our hearts.

★

I TRY NOT TO SPEAK until the dragon reaches the sky, as she begins a long journey south. Our ascent is done, and we're flying. It is just as extraordinary the second time around, but I stay quiet, letting Marley experience all of it without my voice interrupting. I cannot wait to hear his amazement. He is saying nothing right now, and I know it's because of the wonder of it all, the unbelievable—

He leans over the side of the dragon and throws up.

"Yikes, Marley!" I shout, giving him a look of sympathy.

"Dragon-sickness," he says queasily. "Who knew?"

There is an awkward beat of silence, and then we both laugh. Even Blue makes a chuffing noise.

"So tell me," Marley finally says, "what are we doing when we get home? What's the plan?"

I've never been the best at plans. I tend to act upon impulse and make it up as I go. Whenever I have homework, I leave it until the night before and use the panic of the deadline to fuel my writing.

"Don't have a plan," I tell him honestly. "But Freddy's emails have been a bit odd. I just want to get the lay of the land. Check in with Erica. Murrey, too."

"We must be careful. Portia had people with her when she came to Saint Giles. The whole room was under her spell pretty quickly."

"We'll be careful."

"*I'll* be careful—you could go running off after moving statues and getting yourself into all kinds of trouble."

"Yeah, yeah."

The speed of the dragon in the air allows us to reach Edinburgh and the River Forth in an hour. I whisper instructions to Blue as she circles in the sky like an airplane. I use the three massive bridges as my bearings and soon spot Inchkeith.

We land.

I dismount, feeling strange. It's like visiting a memory. The island I came to when I wanted to save Marley is quiet and darkened. The kelpies are nowhere around, and neither is the all-powerful witch who saved me.

She is back in Loch Ness, more of a stranger to me than ever.

"Look," Marley gasps, and I realize what he must've spotted before I even see it for myself. "It's . . . him."

Ren. Lavrentiy. Marley's almost-stepfather, who turned out to be a siren. Opal turned him to stone, right here, when they fought. I saw her do it. She gave him a chance, but he squandered it.

His stone form lies on the rubble just ahead of us, covered in greenery. I watch Marley walk slowly toward him. He didn't see it happen at the time.

Now he can see the remains of a man he deeply cared about, spell or no spell.

I watch my cousin reach out and touch the stone statue's cheek reverently.

"You okay?" I ask quietly.

He is silent for a few minutes, just staring into the statue's face. Then, "Do you think any of it was real?

Do you think the good parts were actually good or just the bad parts all dressed up?"

I consider the question. I didn't know Ren the way Marley did. "I'm not sure, Marley."

He nods solemnly. "I wish your heart could match up with your head when it comes to bad people. I know he was bad. I know he didn't love us. He was using us to get to your parents. My head hates that, thinks he's terrible. Thinks it's right to see him like this."

I sniff. "But the heart . . ."

Marley bows his head, and his face crumples for a moment. I see the tear hit the ground, a gray droplet against the gravel. I watch his small hand stretch across Ren's large one, made of stone.

"You forgive him?" I prompt, stunned by this display, after everything.

"Of course," Marley whispers. "I hate thinking of him here. All alone."

I force myself to turn away, staring at the wide flowing river. "We need to get across." I turn to the dragon, suddenly realizing that I don't know how to address her directly.

"Blue?"

The dragon's great head rises, and she snorts in approval of the name.

"Nice," I say. "Can you swim across the Forth? With us on your back?"

I'm amazed at her intelligence, shown not only in the way she understands language but also in her eyes. She moves to the water, and I mount up once more.

"Marley, let's go," I say carefully. "We don't have a lot of time."

Marley stares at Ren for a moment longer and then steps away, joining me on Blue's back. We wince as our feet brush the cold water, Blue slithering toward Edinburgh with us perched upon her back, the only part of her exposed out of the water.

Marley watches Ren until he is no longer in sight and we have reached the banks of the city. Neither of us speaks as we dismount onto familiar land.

"Stay here, stay hidden," I tell Blue. "We'll be back; I'll use the water to call you."

Her eyes blink slowly and she vanishes into the depths. I glance around, half expecting to see kelpies, but there are no signs of any. I find it strange but say nothing, not wanting to voice the concern I feel.

It doesn't take long to reach the city. But it is different. Dramatically so. The streets are dead, completely deserted. The windows and living rooms in every house are dark, despite it being the evening and not early morning. The streetlamps aren't lit.

"What's happened here?" I breathe.

"I told you," Marley replies. "She's here."

The feeling of unease turns into one of dread as we make our way farther into town. My walk becomes brisker before finally morphing into a run, Marley doing the same. I'm headed for the Old Town.

We arrive and it confirms my worst fear. Something is badly wrong. There are no people, let alone Hidden Folk. The shops are shut up.

Then I see him.

Greyfriars Bobby. A little bronze statue of a dog who once taught me that magic was real and changed everything. He watches me from the top of Candlemaker Row, his bronze tail wagging just a little.

Marley can't see him, but I follow. He leads us to the exact same spot as the first time we met: Avizandum, a bookshop.

I knock while Marley glances around, looking to the entrance of the kirk and down the steep winding street we stand upon. I can hear cautious movement on the other side of the door. Then the latch is lifted, and a pair of frightened eyes stare out.

"Erica?"

The Hulder is relieved to see that it's us, and she quickly ushers us inside.

"What are you doing in Avizandum? What's happened?" I demand as soon as we're safely inside.

She checks to make sure the door is double-locked.

"This place is a ghost town," Marley says as she lights some candles. "What's going on?"

“Sit,” Erica says. “I’ll tell you everything, sit down.”

As the candles are lit, the rest of the bookshop is illuminated, and both Marley and I start as we realize there are many Hidden Folk pressed up against the walls and seated upon the floor. They are exhausted and defeated.

“Erica, what’s going on?” I demand, staring at all their accusing faces.

“Everything has gone wrong,” she finally says, her voice heavy and jaded. “Portia is hunting every last one of us. She’s caught plenty.”

My eyes scan the room, and my heart seizes up in pain. “Where’s—”

“Murrey was the first to be taken,” she says, reading my thoughts. “Nobody has seen him.”

I feel their glares as I take in this horrific news.

“Sit down, Ramya,” Erica pleads. “And we’ll tell you. But it’s not good. Not good at all.”

CHAPTER TWELVE

PRODIGAL SON

The Hidden Folk are too exhausted to Glamour, so I watch as Marley takes in their appearances. The pointed ears and tails, the claws and fangs. He visibly swallows as the full scale of their difference is laid clear before him.

"It's all right," I say under my breath, and he nods shakily, letting me know he's heard me. We sit down by the counter at the front of the bookshop, and Erica checks the windows.

"There's a hex on these," she says quietly. "No one can see in, only out."

I'm about to reply when she violently shushes me.

The whole room grows even more tense, and I can see why. Outside, in the dark and rainy street, two faeries are making their way toward Candlemaker

Row, toward the shop. Marley and I stay completely still and silent, as does every Hidden creature in the room. The first of the two faeries stops to peer through the window, frowning slightly. I am holding my breath in terror, half expecting him to try to smash the glass.

I feel a crackling in my hand, and I look down to see a small bolt spitting and sizzling upon my palm, an electrical charge just waiting to be shot at something. Or someone. Marley and Erica see it too, and both noticeably react.

"What are you going to do?" Erica whispers.

I watch as the fae take one final glance inside, and then they move away. Only when they've been out of sight for thirty seconds do I close my palm into a fist, extinguishing the spark.

"You've been learning?" Erica asks, her voice full of relief.

"Yeah," I say, suddenly feeling a little ashamed of the lack of studying I've been doing. I was so focused on getting back to Edinburgh, I never thought about them needing me to be really good at magic. "Kind of."

"What's happened here?" Marley presses.

"Portia's invaded," Erica says bleakly. "She's got the humans under curfew and mostly staying out of the streets. We don't fully know how. She's got the fae on her side, as you saw."

We all turn back to the windows, and I shudder.

"Why has she taken Murrey?" I ask, feeling rage seep in as I say the words.

Another troll moves a little closer. "We don't exactly have a direct line to Portia. She hasn't communicated with any of us. But the fae appear randomly to round up Hidden Folk."

"My guess," Erica says loftily, "is that, because most Hidden Folk are far less susceptible to sirens than humans, she wants us gone. Out of the way, or at least kept from the humans. She needs them compliant."

"This is creepy," I utter, peering back out into the gloomy, unlit street. "How has she done this in such a short time?"

"We don't know. Television?"

"Maybe. That was why Ren was sidling up to my family—because Mum and Dad were on morning television. However, Portia seems cleverer than Ren."

"Where is the rest of your coven?" the troll asks.

"All over the place," Marley replies. "Gran is who knows where, Aunt Cass and Uncle Mike are in London, and—"

"Marley," I say, cutting him off. I cannot explain why, but nothing feels safe, even in here. We should not be gabbing about our family. My face tells him as much.

"So you're all taking cover in here?" I ask, examining the faces huddled inside the Stranger's bookshop. "All day?"

"The fae obviously know to find most of us in the Grassmarket," says a sprite, speaking with a small and crestfallen voice from atop a pile of law books. "They trashed most of the stalls."

"The back door here leads to the Grassmarket," I point out, remembering my last time in here, with the Stranger. "Are you sure this is safe?"

"The tunnel was blocked off; we don't know by whom. We're safe for now."

I consider the possibility that the Stranger may have blocked it off, to give them a safe place. As ever, I'm bitter that he is not here. Just as he wasn't there when I needed him at Inchkeith. We scraped our way out of that disaster, but I'm feeling far less confident now that I'm huddled in his shop with some terrified Hidden Folk.

"We have to break Murrey out of wherever she's got him," I say, my voice low and deep and angry. Murrey may be a vampire, a creature that stories will call fearsome and wicked, but he is one of the gentlest people I have ever known—second only to Marley. "Where's she keeping him?"

"We don't know, none of us do," another Hulder says. "Anyone who stands up to the fae . . ."

She does not need to finish the sentence.

"Where's Freddy?" I ask, turning back to Erica. "Have you seen him?"

"Barely," she says. "But I have his address. Hidden Folk wouldn't dare go there, but you—"

"Write it down for me," I say, getting to my feet and nodding at Marley. He also stands while Erica dashes to the shop counter, snatching a scrap of paper and a pen. As she scribbles, I take another glance outside and onto the street.

"You're lucky," Erica finally says, handing over the address, "to have powers. To have any power. Use it for the people in this room."

She gives me a stern look, one that makes me want to glance away. I take the scrap of paper and mutter my thanks before slipping out of the shop, Marley in my wake.

"Where are we headed?" he asks, and I flinch at how silent the street is. No cars, no people, no revelers coming out of Frankenstein's or ghost tours visiting the kirk. I read the address to him, and he takes the paper from me.

"We can go past the flat," he says quietly.

"Marley."

He stops, a few steps ahead of me. He did hear me say his name, but he doesn't turn around. I don't feel brave enough to say what I'm thinking, so we set off in silence, down Candlemaker Row to the edge of the Grassmarket, the human one that's aboveground. Aunt Leanna's shop, and the flat she and Marley lived in, are there.

We are the only people around as we stand before it. The window is broken, a shattered comet upon the glass. The interior is ransacked and dark. I grab Marley's hand and we stand there, just staring at it.

"I hate them," he finally says. Soft. The lightest touch of venom.

"I know," I say back.

"I'm tired of all this. Of living with their bullying."

"I know," I repeat. "But we need to find Freddy. We can't stay here."

"Who says he's on our side? He's a siren."

"Marley." The reproach in my voice is fragile. "Come on. We can't do that."

"Do what, use common sense?"

"It's not common sense to say someone is bad because of what they are. He can't help what he is. He's always been a good friend to us."

If things were less serious, Marley would normally make a joke about me and Freddy fancying each other, but he doesn't. For once, I miss the teasing. Things feel so heavy all of a sudden.

"Let's go, then," he says dejectedly.

So we leave, heading for the New Town address. We leave behind the shop with so many amazing memories of our family, now ransacked and broken.

*

"I DON'T WANT TO GO IN."

Marley states this as we stand on the doorstep of a house by the water. The one Erica's scrap of paper has led us to. I stare at him.

"Why?"

Marley kicks a stone along the street and shrugs. "Just don't want to see him."

"It's dangerous for you to be on—"

"I'll be fine. I'll be with Blue. Whistle if you need us."

"Marley—"

He is already setting off down the street, in the direction of where we left Blue. I watch him go, a little horrified. I envision some of the fae snatching him up. I'm about to call his name when I remember just how dead and empty the streets have become. My voice will echo, and I instinctively know that this is not a good thing.

I knock instead. I'm vaguely aware of how timid a knock it is. Lacking the urgency that this increasingly serious situation needs.

Freddy opens the door regardless, completely shocked to see me.

"Can I come in?"

"Ramya?" His blond hair is tousled, and he's wearing an oversized black hoodie and blue jeans.

It's bizarre because I am so used to seeing him in a crisp private-school uniform.

I wait for him to usher me indoors, but he doesn't move. We stare at each other.

"You didn't tell me things were this bad," I finally say.

"I know," he replies softly. "Come in. But you can't stay long."

I frown, following him into the house. It's so similar to my parents' home in Stockbridge that I feel slightly unnerved. Freddy leads me into the front room, and I head straight for the white door in the far corner of the parlor. It opens to reveal a hidden closet, just like the one in our house.

"I had one of these," I tell him dazedly. "Used to hide in it for hours, waiting for Mum and Dad to get really panicked and worried."

"Did they?"

I close the door slowly. "No."

"I'm sorry I didn't tell you everything. But I knew you would do this."

"Do what?"

"Come charging down here, trying to fix things, and you really need to stay in Loch Ness."

"There are fae working for Portia in Loch Ness. They're searching for something."

"Your house is protected, though?"

"Yes."

"Ramya, listen. There's something I've been meaning to tell you."

Before he can go any further, a car pulls up outside. I can't see it, as the curtains are closed, but I can hear it—especially with the quiet of the street. I turn back to Freddy and freeze when I see terror cross his face. I open my mouth, but I'm being bundled into the closet we were just examining.

"What?" I snap as he closes the door on me.

"Stay in there, stay out of sight," he pleads, his voice, which holds so much power over other people, now full of fear and terror. "Please, Ramya."

I stare out of the microscopic crack in the door, and I'm about to ask what is going on when I hear the front door open. Freddy dives to the sofa, flopping down onto it and trying to be as nonchalant as possible. He whips out his mobile phone and starts scrolling.

The living room door opens, and I stifle a gasp as I see who is entering.

Portia.

She is exactly as she was when I was six. When we last saw each other in person. She is wearing shimmery tights and a gray work dress. She kicks off a pair of black heels with blood-red undersides.

"Evening," she says to Freddy.

I almost scream when I see what she does next. She bends down and presses a kiss to his mussed blond hair.

The realization hits me like a sledgehammer to the temple.

Freddy is Portia's son.

And I'm trapped in their living room wall.

CHAPTER THIRTEEN

THE WHY

I'm shaking and silently enraged as I watch Portia sit down next to Freddy and start massaging her right foot with her hands.

"How was your last day of term?" she asks him calmly.

"Fine," Freddy replies flatly. "Not much fun with everyone rushing to get home before curfew."

"The curfew is at eight," she says, rolling her eyes. "You can get up to all sorts of fun before then."

"We have different ideas of fun."

Portia throws him a sideways glance. "You're missing your little friend."

Freddy is careful to show no reaction. "Yes."

"No one wants the two of you to be reunited more than me."

He leaps to his feet and walks toward the bay window. "Don't."

"Trust me, darling, you don't want a friend who is immune to your powers. Where's the fun in that? I've done it once, never again."

"You're not using me to get to Ramya."

I feel like growling at the mention of my name. I'm slowly beginning to wonder if Marley was right. Perhaps Freddy is untrustworthy. Then again, he is the only thing standing between me and Portia right now, and he's giving nothing away to her.

"You think the little witch is your friend, but she hates us," Portia tells him softly. I frown at the words. I hate her, not Freddy. "She won't ever forgive what you are."

I look to Freddy, but I can't see his face through the gap in the wood.

"That's my problem, not yours."

"She was quite the little surprise all those years ago," Portia muses. "Stubborn."

"She still is."

"I didn't really give her a moment's thought until Lavrentiy sent me that letter. He may have botched all of that up, but he worked out what she was. What she's going to be."

"Mum," Freddy says. I brace myself, waiting for him to give me up.

"Yes?"

"Please leave my friends alone. I don't know what all of this is for, but—"

"It's for you."

"No, it's not."

"It is!" She gets to her feet, glaring at his back with an expression that reminds me of my own mother. "The world was slipping. Is slipping. Soon it's going to be very unfriendly for boys like you."

"You don't know me, Mum. Please don't pretend any of this is for me. You want power. You've been fidgeting about in London for years while I rot up here, and now that I finally have a life—"

"Rot? Is that what you call a beautiful house and a world-class education? Do you know how many prime ministers were educated at your school? One more when you graduate."

"I'm not going to be your political puppet; you've had enough of those."

"And what a bore they all were. So unimaginative. It's not even fun after a while. Of course, you would *know* that if you ever—"

"I don't like what we are," Freddy says sadly. "I don't like what you do. What's the plan, then, Mum? Keep them all scared and locked up like cattle?"

"Precisely. They behave, they stay in line, they buy lots of things. It's perfect. Darling, the rules aren't for you, don't get so worked up. You're free to do—"

"And the Hidden Folk?"

Freddy glances at me, almost imperceptibly. I realize that he's making her talk for my benefit. Portia's mask slips as he says the words, and something ugly enters her expression.

"They're all due for extinction," she finally murmurs. "Vampires in libraries, Hulders still cleaning hearths, only this time in some Grassmarket pub. Sprites curled up in bookshops. They've outstayed their evolutionary welcome, Freddy. They're useless. Cozying up to humans in the hopes that one day they can release their Glamour and be accepted. It's obscene."

I lean back within the closet, as far as I can go. My back presses gently against the wall and my knees feel cramped, all pushed up against the door. I'm finding it difficult to process what I am hearing.

"Freddy, I had to work and practice to get to this point," Portia tells him, and I can see that her eyes are shining. "You have so much more of a gift. I've seen your influence over people. You're beyond me *now*, let alone when I was your age."

I'm angered at how human she seems. I've kept her in my head all these years: the perfect nightmare of a person who has no positive qualities. Seeing her with Freddy shakes that image, and I don't like it. I don't want to believe that, deep down in the dungeons of their souls, people I have labeled as bad can have damp raindrops of good.

"I don't want this curse," Freddy says, and it's so quiet, I barely hear him. "I don't want to be like you. I don't want this life."

"Oh, sweetheart." Portia says it with resignation, and it makes the electricity in my hands spark and pulse. "I used to feel that way."

"No, you didn't."

"Yes, I did. Freddy." She is imploring him, her guard down and her eyes wide. "I wanted to help everyone. Every person I met, I tried to influence them for good. I tried to steer them onto the path that would serve them. But these people? They don't want what's best for them, Freddy. They want to be ordered. They don't want to choose."

"You're not even lying to yourself, you're just lying to me," Freddy says dejectedly. "You know what you're saying is complete tar, but you think I'm stupid enough to let you lay it all over me."

Her face hardens. "It's the truth. They want someone telling them what to do."

"Maybe. If it's in their best interests."

"And what's that?" I watch Portia cross the room, until she is standing right in front of Freddy. "Want to hear a story?"

Her voice is soft and feathery, but it makes Freddy alert. He stares into her face and says nothing.

"The very first siren to walk out of the sea lived in the woods," she says. She sounds melodic and gentle, but I can see that Freddy is just as unnerved as I am. "She lived in a cottage, not too far from two others. Both humans, in their own little houses. One human noticed that a chicken was missing from his garden. He asked the siren. She told him she had seen the second man with the first's chicken. He had locked it in his shed. The first man demanded that the second man hand over the key. He refused. They fought, and the first man killed the second. He found no key, though."

"I don't want to hear this story," Freddy mutters, his face and knuckles whitening.

"A new neighbor moved in, and the first man grew jealous of his bountiful garden," Portia goes on, unfazed. "He cried out at night, 'How should he have such a garden and not I?' Well, the siren told him that the second man chained himself to his front door each morning. With a beautiful golden chain that brought prosperity and good luck. The first man hungrily demanded a chain for himself. Why should the other man have a beautiful chain when he had none at all?"

I can feel my breathing getting a little more frantic, and I no longer force myself to quiet down. I'm glaring at her through the crack in the door and shaking with the force of the adrenaline.

"The man could not escape his chain. He grew to resent it. He cried out for it to be unlocked. But he had no key. He begged the siren to help, but she could not. For the second man had the key to all the chains, she said. The first man howled and cursed the second. How dare he, with his fine garden, rob others of their freedom. Of their rightful bounty. He died on the floor of his cottage, hungry and thirsty, chained to his own front door and reaching out for a key he could not see."

Freddy and I both watch as she reaches beneath the collar of her dress to withdraw a long chain necklace.

Instead of a pendant, there is a slim golden key. She holds it up, and it gleams.

"You have to make them think the chains are their idea," she says serenely. "And that someone else wants to hold the key from them. Then you will be free. You and only you."

Silence follows her story and her revelation of the golden key.

"Hidden Folk are mostly immune to us," she says, adding a coda to her frightening display. "But humans are not. They all follow us. They all believe us. It will be more so for you. They will never disobey or deny you, Freddy, so you must be ready to create and inflict order. Distraction. All of them are compelled to worship us, so let them."

Freddy's expression changes, and a touch of triumph enters his face. "Not all of them, Mum. She's different. She'll never be under your thumb."

He's talking about me, and it makes my nerves twitch, but then I notice how spiky and unsure Portia now seems. It gives me a taste of the same triumph, and a tiny shot of strength.

"I told you, son," she finally says. "She will never accept you. Not really. I promise you that. I had a friend just like her."

"You've never had friends."

"I had a thousand lives before you were born. But only one true friend, and even that ended in ugliness. It always does, it always will."

"Were they like Ramya? Were they immune?"

I watch Portia, expecting her to deny it. She does not. Her memories are with the ghost of this other person, this friend. Whoever she's talking about, there are clearly things that she feels but does not want to say.

"All of this is for the best," she settles on, speaking with the same calm serenity that she tried to use on me all those years ago. "And you can tell your little friend something from me. I'd love for her to pay me a visit. She would be in no danger. I just want to make her a nice offer. And the longer she refuses, the weaker that vampire gets."

Freddy's eyes widen and then dart to my hiding spot unconsciously.

"You can come out now, Ramya," Portia says composedly. "Let's talk, you and I. It's been so long since we last saw each other."

CHAPTER FOURTEEN

DRESS REHEARSAL

I wish teleportation were one of my gifts. Yet even Aunt Opal is incapable of that. I hesitate and then swiftly exit the closet, not wanting Portia to come in after me. I slam the door behind me and straighten my stance, staring at the female siren. Our first meeting since that party in my parents' London house. When she deliberately caused a rift in the family and my grandfather left forever.

She looks me up and down, almost hungrily. I was expecting hatred and resentment, but she is mildly fascinated instead. "You're so much taller."

I don't respond. Instead, I flex my hands. They crackle and spit with electricity. The rage and the pain of the last few years build in me, making the current stronger. A part of me detaches, floats away from my body, and settles in the highest corner of the ceiling. It stares down at the three of us and casually wonders if I have enough electricity in my hands to kill her. It wonders what will happen if I throw a blast of magic at her.

All the remaining parts of me have to fight not to listen to it.

"Easy now," Portia says carefully. "Let's just—"

"Your voice doesn't work on me," I say brokenly.

The adrenaline is mixed with memory and emotion, stripping me raw. "Not like it did on him. I never saw him again, by the way. After what you did."

Her eyes flicker as they flash between me and Freddy. "Is that so?" Her gaze drops to my hands once more. "So it's true. You really are getting stronger."

"Yeah," I snap. "I am. And I'm also the only one in this room with a power that works over the other person. So step away from the door."

"Ramya," she says, and while her voice doesn't control me, it does affect me. It sounds so reasonable. "All I've been trying to do is talk to you. I think you're fantastic. I think your magic is—"

"Don't listen to her, Ramya," Freddy says quickly. "She's lying."

"I'm not," she fires back, still looking at me. "You're a little anomaly. Special. I can see it; I saw it all those years ago." She focuses intently on me and lowers her voice to a deep and compelling timbre. "Sit down."

I don't move. It's her testing me again. Gauging my susceptibility.

"No."

"Incredible," she breathes. "What a gift, Ramya. Or a curse, perhaps."

I glower. "Having a mind of your own is not a curse."

"Ah," she sighs, smiling wanly at me. "Yes. When you're thirteen, maybe. But just wait. Wait until the world becomes too much, too wearisome. Wait until you have a million responsibilities crushing down upon you. Then you'll wish for someone like me. Someone who will make the difficult decisions and decide what is best for you."

"Is that what you think you're doing?" Freddy asks from behind me.

"It's what I know I'm doing, sweetheart," she replies, not breaking her eye contact with me. "No one wants freedom if it means chaos. People crave order. That's all I'm doing. You understand that, Ramya? That brain of yours, it feels muddled a lot of the time, does it not? Wouldn't you love it to feel smoother? To feel just like everybody else?"

I throw my hand out before me and let everything Opal has taught me, as well as a dash of instinct, shoot out of my fingertips. Portia's golden chain snaps and breaks, the key flying free of her neck and shooting toward me. I grasp it between my fingers for a millisecond before throwing it onto their front room floor. I blast it with as much fire as I'm able to muster, knowing Mum and Opal would do a better job.

But I'm the only witch here. I'm the only representative of my coven here, the only one who bothered to come, to face the siren who tried to destroy all of us. So I blast it with every bit of emotion. I let the hungry, snarling feeling of rage and the need for revenge take over.

The thing is, when I've finished and we're all just staring at this small pile of darkened ash and coughing against the smoke, I don't feel better.

I feel nothing.

I look back up at Portia. "What have you done with Murrey?"

I'm sick of her talking, but I need answers.

"Ah, your little vampire friend," she says, moving nonchalantly toward a phone that is positioned neatly on an end table. She lifts the receiver and daintily dials a number. She doesn't put the phone to her ear, however, but lays it flat upon the table.

I glare at it, wondering what her game is. "Where is he? Tell me before I start feeling like bursting the pipes in this place."

"What a little brute your family have made you into," Portia muses.

"Where. Is. Murrey?"

The last of her pretend niceness slips away. She clearly knows I'm a lost cause. Cunning, wily vindictiveness spreads across her face, and she licks her lips in anticipation of her words. "You'll never see him alive again unless I get what I want, Ramya."

I can feel my intakes of breath quickening, becoming too short. "The fae, up north. They're hunting something for you."

She smirks. "Sure. Hand it over and I'll let your friends go."

"Why do you want her?"

"Her?"

I freeze. "It. Why do you want it?"

She splays her hands out collectedly. "I'm building myself a little council. All I want to do is make the trains run on time and clear out some of the trash. If my adored son over there won't help me, I need a little crew who will. And there's something in Loch Ness I would so desperately love to have. It's a nice little hub of magic up there. I'd like a slice of it on my side."

The front door crashes open, and three members of the fae are suddenly standing behind Portia, ready to attack or defend upon command. While their entrance was abrupt, there is nothing clumsy about them. They are slick and precise, showing a dexterity of movement I will never have, no matter how hard I try.

That same twitching, prickly anger starts to pulse in my hands again. One faerie notices, and a flash of unease crosses her face. She glances at the back of Portia's head, and whatever she tells herself internally, it steadies her nerve.

"Let me out," I say, calmly enough. "You don't want to know how I got here today."

Portia's piercing blue eyes are amused as she stares down at me. She knows that while I have magic and she does not, she has power. This city is under her control, purely based on the sway of her voice. Freddy and Erica once told me that sirens had one true weakness. They were incapable of working together. They do not form a secret society or a collective group, like a coven, because they prefer being alone. They can't control one another, therefore they do not ally with one another. They act alone and choose chaos and power when it suits them. Portia just happens to be the first known siren in my lifetime to convince other Hidden Folk to help her.

I eye the fae.

"Careful of this witch," one of them says. "I've heard about her. Water trickery—"

"Shut up," Portia interrupts coolly. "Ramya knows not to do anything silly. Don't you, dear?"

I force my face to mirror her unruffled expression. I raise my palms. I fight a slightly foggy and emotional brain to plunge deep and remember what Opal has taught me. I close my eyes, and suddenly all I hear is tinnitus. I feel the energy pulse and push, like a shoal of fish trying to break free from a net.

"Heads up, Freddy," I hiss. Then I release it all.

Behind me, the bay window suddenly smashes. The tiny fragments of glass break apart, causing a sound loud enough to make the fae flinch and leap back.

Portia's composure slips. She cries out and covers her eyes, but I don't send the shards flying toward her. I let them drop, pushing by Freddy to mount the windowsill.

"Hey," he says quickly as I raise my fingertips to my lips, about to whistle. "I'm on your side. But it's not safe for you here. I'll search for Murrey. I promise."

We look at each other as I crouch in the broken window. I glance back at Portia, who is getting to her feet, ready to pounce.

I whistle. Loudly, shrilly, and with a strong screech of urgency. I clamber out into the street, careful not to step on the broken glass.

"Grab her!" Portia shrieks, thumping one of her henchmen on the arm. They dive for the window, but Freddy bars their path. I throw him a grimace of gratitude and whistle again.

"Come on, Marley," I breathe. "Like we said."

Then I hear it. The swooping, sweeping sound of great wings. A dark shape ahead in the fog grows closer, larger, and more distinct. It is perhaps a good thing at this very moment that the citizens of Edinburgh are locked away under curfew and under a spell, otherwise they would glance out of their living room windows to see a vast, intimidating blue dragon standing on their cobblestoned street.

"Is . . . is that . . . ?" Freddy babbles, staring up at Blue.

He is agonized by disbelief.

"Let me introduce you all to my *dragon*, Portia!" I shout, almost feverish with triumph.

One of the fae screams, a terrified sound that is almost too high for human ears to hear. Portia gazes at the dragon, with Marley astride it, and her hand slowly moves to cover her mouth.

Blue seems to fixate on the two sirens and proceeds to let out a great roar. Portia's hair blows back, and she staggers to grab the frame of the window. Freddy curses, covering his ears, but he also manages to look impressed.

Marley wastes no time, leaning down to haul me up onto Blue. I settle into a saddle that is not there and lock eyes with my only siren friend.

"Call me when your mum's not around."

He laughs, still mystified by Blue.

"A dragon," another one of the fae gasps. "It can't be. A real dragon. But they—I thought they were all gone."

Curious. Blue is perhaps not the creature they have been searching for, then.

We don't wait around to ask. Blue uses the street to take flight, and we're soaring high into the fog, leaving a wicked siren, her decidedly not-wicked son, and the fae behind. I am only half relieved, though. As we fly, I glance back down and think of Murrey. Murrey and all the other Hidden Folk and humans stuck under her tyranny.

And I feel ashamed.

CHAPTER FIFTEEN

DEAD MAN'S PARTY

It's Marley's birthday, and Aunt Leanna is in her element.

How we made it back to the house without the aunts knowing that we fled to Edinburgh for the night, I don't fully know. Alona was not there to help us sneak back in, so I had to fly us. It was awkward and painful, and we barely made it through the window without waking up the rest of the family.

The four of us are having lunch in the sunny part of the house. Leanna casts some kind of warming spell. It is still December, after all. We are eating coronation chicken sandwiches with fizzy drinks and chocolate cake.

Aunt Leanna has spurned the green vegetables for once, and it's wonderful.

Until I remember. Until everything I saw in Edinburgh comes flooding back into my memory. The huddled, frightened faces of the Hidden Folk. Freddy's exhaustion and worry. Portia's calculating words.

Murrey.

It feels wrong for us to be sitting here, safe and having a lovely time, while all that is happening elsewhere. I have to formulate a plan, but Freddy sent an adamant email this morning, begging me to stay away.

Not that I have ever been good at doing what I'm told.

Everyone is talking and eating while I sit here feeling fuzzy. Dyspraxia doesn't just affect my physical body, it also affects speech, and right now I am finding it difficult to communicate. Words seem faded and hard for my tongue to grip. It's a groggy, disorienting feeling. I used to get it during the afternoon at school. I would sometimes stare at the wall above the clock and feel as though my brain were filling up with water.

"Ramya?" Opal says my name.

"Mm?"

"We're getting the cake out. Don't you want any?" I realize that their laughter and conversation have actually been absent for some time. My brain was just not processing them. I feel as if I'm a signal that has delayed, putting me about thirty seconds behind everybody else. It's maddening, and it makes me want to pull at my own hair. I don't often slip out of control like this; I imagine it's because I used a lot of magic with Portia.

I'm overstimulated and overwhelmed, and I don't like having to pretend that everything is just fine when it is not. When Freddy is basically trapped, Murrey is missing, and the Hidden Folk are being hounded.

"When are we going back to Edinburgh?"

My voice is a little scratchy, but I manage to get the words out and in the correct order, with just enough steel in my tone—enough to let them know that I'm really serious about this.

Opal watches me before pointedly cutting a sliver of chocolate birthday cake and placing it in front of me. "Eat something."

"When"—I ignore her command—"are we going back to Edinburgh, Aunt Opal? We've been hidden out here long enough. It's time to go back."

"Ramya." Aunt Leanna speaks, and it is in a tone of voice I have never heard from her. It's stern and terse and without her usual warmth. "Your mum and dad are not away for a relaxing spa holiday. They are working, with your aunt Opal and me, on a carefully laid plan. Part of that carefully laid plan involves the two of you staying here, where you're safe."

"Safe for how long?" I snap. "Until they've completely taken over the lowlands and they start making their way up here? There's fae already about. Plus, Marley saw something strange."

"Ramya!" Marley cries, making a gesture that begs me to be quiet.

"What did you see?" Opal asks my cousin.

"Nothing," Marley insists, getting flustered. "I thought I saw . . . something, but I couldn't have."

"He saw Grandpa."

Leanna buries her face in her hands, and Opal stares at me. The words are not even fully out of my mouth before she begins shaking her head.

"That's not possible."

"That's what I said," I reply. "But Marley says—"

"I was probably imagining it," Marley interjects, glaring at me. "Of course it wasn't really him."

I narrow my eyes. "Then why did you—"

"There is no such thing as ghosts."

The voice that speaks does not belong to any of us.

We all swivel to look at the doorframe. Standing in it, with his hand raised as if to knock, is the Stranger. He is wearing tiny black sunglasses and is peering at us over the top of them.

"How did you get inside the house?" I exclaim in distaste.

He smiles and shrugs. "There is no magic older than I am."

I turn to my aunts, expecting them to be appalled or confused, but they are relieved to see him. I can't understand why. He's always a bystander. Other than passing along my grandfather's mission and occasionally leading me to magical bookshops, he has done nothing to help us against the sirens. Nothing that I can see, at least.

"Marley." The Stranger speaks directly to my cousin, something I can sense he finds unnerving. "What did you see?"

Marley gazes around at all of us, and I can tell that he's weighing whether to continue his pretense. He settles on the truth.

"I saw it by the loch. It was just like Grandpa. Not pale or shimmery like a ghost. It was just him. Real. In the flesh."

"When was this?" Leanna asks, frowning.

"I didn't see it, but Marley was really spooked," I pipe up, cutting Leanna off and steering the conversation away from us being by the loch without their knowledge.

"I don't know what it could've been," Marley says, almost apologetically. He is afraid to look the Stranger in the eye.

“It’s all right,” the Stranger says quietly. “I believe you.”

The words are like an enchantment over Marley. He is invigorated, in such a way that I feel guilty for doubting him.

“But it can’t be him,” Marley says, more to himself than to us. “It just—”

“It can’t be him,” the Stranger concurs, speaking softly. “I’m sorry. I know how that hurts. But nothing, no spell, can bring humans back from the dead.”

I glance across at him, puzzled. “Humans?”

“Come on,” Aunt Leanna says chipperly. “Show us where you saw it.”

★

THE FIVE OF US WALK in the chilled air, with Marley leading the way. I glance behind me, sullen at seeing the Stranger and Opal walking side by side, with their arms linked and heads close together. Whispering.

“You have to share your aunt.”

Aunt Leanna says it to me, kindly and under her breath.

“I just don’t see why they’re so friendly,” I mutter, lashing out at a twig with a kick.

“You and your aunt are so similar,” Leanna says.

"When you decide to be pleasant, when you let your guard down, everyone within ten miles wants to be your closest friend."

I stop in my tracks and stare at her. "I'm not like that."

"Oh, yes, you are. Or could be." Leanna wraps an arm around me. "What's going on with you, chicken?"

"Other than the sirens announcing a war on witches? Nothing."

"It's not a child's job to save the world, Rams."

"Well, then tell me what you're all planning."

Marley reaches his old spot by the edge of the loch and points ahead. "It was over there."

There is, of course, as we expected, nothing there now. No one scolds him, but I can feel his palpable disappointment. Opal detaches from the Stranger and moves toward the cloudy, dark loch. I watch in fascination as she kneels to touch it, the way I instinctively do when I'm around a large body of water. I suddenly wonder if Blue, or the ceasg, will rise up from the depths. I exchange a glance with Marley, and he is clearly thinking the same thing.

However, it is neither a dragon nor a savage mermaid that rises from the bottom of the large lake.

CHAPTER SIXTEEN

RIPPLES

Opal's touch causes a large, weblike ripple in the water. It spreads to the middle of the loch, and a soft light begins to ascend from beneath. I brace myself, grabbing a rock. I'm ready to hurl it if necessary.

Everyone moves a little closer to Opal, and we all seem to be holding our breath.

Except the Stranger, who does not seem to breathe at all.

The creature that appears on the loch seems as if it's made of water, until it quickly transforms with the speed of someone changing the channel on a television. Suddenly it looks like Opal. The change makes everyone except Opal and the Stranger gasp.

I throw the stone in my hand without even thinking. My aim is pretty horrible. The rock sinks into the lake, a good ten feet from the creature. It watches me, as Opal, then vanishes beneath the surface once more.

"That thing is beyond scary," I say.

"You don't have to throw stones at things that scare you," Opal says over her shoulder.

I glare. "You don't have the ick at the fact that it made itself just like you?"

Opal shrugs. "I'm curious."

The creature reappears, still looking like Opal. It swiftly transforms to reflect me, as if I'm staring into a mirror. Then it tosses the stone back at me. It lands at my feet, an unmistakable challenge.

"What is it?" Leanna asks, aghast.

"You can see it?" I press. Aunt Leanna can't see through Glamour like Opal and I can.

"Yes," she answers. "It . . . looks like you."

My double turns to Leanna when she speaks. The expression on "my" face seems odd to me. Not fully human. It moves a tad closer to Leanna and then switches once again.

Into the image of a man. One I don't know and have never met. Opal instantly straightens, and Leanna lets out a mournful sound before pulling Marley away from the water. I examine her face, and I can see years of sadness lined on it that have never been visible before.

"How can it do this?" Leanna demands, staring desperately at her youngest sister.

Opal shakes her head slightly and stares back at the creature, at the image of the human it's pretending to be. "I don't know this magic."

The Stranger moves into the creature's eyeline, and it instantly vanishes, as if terrified. It seems to become the water, disappearing like a snowflake melting inside a warm palm. I eye the Stranger's back, wondering what it is about him that scared this frightening creature so much.

"What are you?" I ask him, my voice low. He throws me a glance but doesn't answer.

"That's what I saw," Marley confirms. "It must've been pretending to be Grandpa."

I wince at the deep and sincere disappointment in his voice. I forget to ask about who the man was and move toward my cousin instead. I bump shoulders with him, not wanting to show too much affection in front of the adults. I know how he feels, though.

"That must be what Portia has the fae hunting for," I say.

"Mimicry is a kind of trickery I've never known anyone to master," Opal says contemplatively. "It would be useful to her, for sure."

She moves straight to Leanna and briefly hugs her. It's a quick, tight, Opal hug. She doesn't like physical contact for too long. Leanna is clearly grateful for it, swiftly wiping her eyes and setting off toward the house once more. I turn back to Opal and the Stranger, but they're regarding each other as if Marley and I do not exist. The Stranger draws a satin teal pocket square from his pin-striped suit and hands it to my aunt, with an air of importance.

"You'll be needing it," he says.

Opal's face gives nothing away, but she accepts the small scrap of fabric and ties it around her wrist. "I'll take your word for it."

Before I can question the frankly odd interaction, the Stranger is gone. Opal gives Marley a squeeze, and they set off for the house as well.

"Come on," Opal calls back to me. "Stay where I can see you."

I lock eyes with Marley, silently warning him that I will be heading out after bedtime again. He sighs and acknowledges it with a tiny nod. I'm beginning to follow behind the two of them when I spot Alona.

She is distraught, stumbling toward the moonlit side of the loch with great distress.

"Alona!" I call her name, the concern in my voice causing Opal and Marley to spin around. I run toward the dryad, ready to fight for whatever she needs.

"It's my Druid," she says in a splintery voice. "He's gone. And his home has been destroyed."

I turn without hesitation to Opal, who is taking

in Alona's unearthly appearance and her tormented state.

"Where?"

While I'm frustrated with my aunt about a lot of things, I'm grateful to her in this moment. She trusts, she asks the right questions, and she's on our side.

"Take us, let us see," I tell Alona.

She groans out another anguished noise but turns to the path by the water.

We follow.

★

THE DRUID'S COTTAGE IS A saddening sight.

What must've once been a cozy little haven is now ransacked and tattered. Papers ripped and shredded all over the room, the fire deliberately doused and the fabric on the chair destroyed with what had to be a blade. Alona is inconsolable. Marley and I stay with her, flanking her, while Opal searches the little house.

"He's gone," Alona bleats, reaching out toward the destroyed furniture and shattered objects. "They've taken him."

"Who?" Marley asks, but he answers his own question within seconds. "The fae?"

"On Portia's orders, no doubt," I add. "But why him? Does she think he knows about that creature? Or about us?"

"What creature?" Alona asks, bemusement mixing with worry.

"Some weird shape-shifter in the loch," Marley tells her. "We think Portia's after it."

"The siren?"

"Yes."

"So if she gets this shape-shifter thing, she'll let Fog go?"

I turn to Aunt Opal, who rapidly glances away. I can tell that she does not want to make false promises to the dryad.

"He clearly isn't here," I say to Alona, trying to sound positive. "And there're signs of a struggle. Which means they probably took him alive. He's fine, Alona, I'm sure."

"Ramya," Opal murmurs in warning. "Careful."

I suddenly remember what Portia said the night before.

I'm building myself a little council.

"Is Fog quite a powerful Druid?" I ask Alona, trying to sound calm.

"Yes, that's why I don't understand," she responds, sounding tearful. "He's very powerful. I've seen him move boulders. So why didn't he fight them off?"

"Maybe he only intended it to *appear* like a struggle," Opal ponders aloud as she kneels by the hearth to feel how cold the logs in the fire are. "Maybe this is what they want us to see."

Alona is frustrated by this consideration. Even a little angry. "He would never deceive anyone like that."

"Never say never," Opal mutters, getting to her feet. "You don't always know a person."

She looks fleetingly at Alona and then moves into another room. I wait until she is out of earshot and then rush to the dryad.

"We're going back to Edinburgh, with Blue. To-night. Come with us? We can hunt for clues. That's where Portia's based, so if she has your maker, it's probably close to there."

I, maybe a bit selfishly, conceal the fact that I'm more interested in finding Murrey and further investigating the city than I am in tracking down the Druid. However, it's all part of the same plot—to stop Portia from advancing her nasty plan for the Hidden Folk. I told Marley about it as we flew home on Blue. He was silent for some time afterward. Shocked.

Alona's eyes widen at my words, but she nods hurriedly. I step away as Opal returns from the other room.

"Do you have somewhere safe to stay?" she asks Alona.

"Yes," Alona says, a little defensively. "The land. The earth. Everything around here. It was always safe. Until now."

Opal arches an eyebrow at her tone but merely

nods in acknowledgment, saying nothing. We leave the cottage together, closing the door upon the chaos. Alona gives me a meaningful stare, a silent promise to meet us after dark for an adventure, before she transforms into a somehow forlorn-looking tree.

"Now are we going to do something?" I ask Opal.

She touches the teal fabric tied around her wrist and remains silent.

"Ramya's right, Aunt Opal," Marley says. "This is all getting ugly. We can't just do nothing."

"Et tu, Marley?" Opal says dryly.

I clench my jaw but persevere, walking behind her with Marley by my side as we return home. "Why can't you just—"

Opal rounds on me before I have time to say another word, shooting a blast of magic toward me. It hits me right in the sternum, and I'm thrown backward onto the ground. The wind is knocked out of me, and I splutter and swear, trying to get up. I can't. She has bound me somehow, and I struggle against her power. She leans over me, and I expect her to be smug or amused, but she is sad. Sad and angry.

"Get up," she says, in the most strangely sorrowful voice. "Please."

I wrestle against the invisible rope but cannot break free. The more I try, the less I can move and the more agitated I become. I finally give up and release my muscles, glaring up at her.

"Let me go," I gripe, my voice almost a snarl.

"What are you doing?" she says, so softly. "What are you doing, Ramya? Sneaking out every night, waking up too tired to practice magic. What will you do when you come up against someone who *does* practice?"

Wet, warm, and irate tears start to pool, and I can't reach up to swipe them away. I know I shouldn't be too shocked. Of course she knows about the sneaking out; we've been sloppy. Alona's presence and Marley's prior sighting of the weird shape-shifter prove that we haven't been keeping to the garden. I'm certain she doesn't know about Edinburgh and Blue, however. That would really enrage her.

"We just want to help, Aunt Opal," Marley says.

Opal says nothing. Then she releases the spell.

Everything keeping me grounded is gone, and I stagger to my feet. I fire my anger into a spell, blasting it at her. She deflects it with ease, like she's moving a strand of hair out of her face. I throw another, and she does the same. I let out a bellow and cast one final spray of magic. She rebounds it so that it soars back toward me. I duck just in time, missing its impact.

I'm out of breath, and she is as calm as the water in the loch.

"Makes sense," I snap, my eyes still stinging with

salty tears. "I've never been good at anything. Why would magic be any different?"

Opal's face sharpens. "Don't do that. Don't pull the 'woe is me' grift when you've got everything it takes to be outstanding. I won't have it. I'm not that silly school you went to. I expect the best from you because I know you can do it. Do you know how privileged you are to have someone to teach you all this? What did I have? Who did I have? Nothing and no one."

We may not be only speaking of magic now.

It's difficult to breathe. Usually, when someone backs me into a corner, I get to tell myself a little story. I tell myself that they don't understand, that the complexities of me are specific only to me and I share nothing with anyone. In the story, I am the hero, and they're all the villains. Anything I do is acceptable because they are bad. Doing bad things to bad people is a loophole in the Golden Rule, I tell myself. I don't look too closely at that; I don't let it interrupt the flow of my narrative.

But I can't do any of that with Opal. She is like me. A witch like me. Neurodivergent like me. She knows what it means to find the sun too blistering while others beg for it to be hotter. She winces at louder sounds, hates public transport and the feeling of buttons. She speaks directly and doesn't bother with the hidden subtleties that neurotypical people like so much. She has a social battery that runs out just as rapidly as mine does. She struggles with communication. Her balance is fragile. Her brain is a brilliant, busy hive of a thing with thousands of years of taking the high road and ignoring the jeers and being the better person.

She is made like me, and she has never for a second let anyone back her into a corner for it. She is loyal. She is stoic. She is everything I want to be.

I think I've been telling lies. Not just to her and Mum and Aunt Leanna. But to myself.

"Look at your cousin," Opal says despairingly.

I do. I turn to Marley. He is worn out and pale.

"Why don't you think for a moment about what he saw earlier?" she adds. "When that creature transformed. Why don't you ask him if he's all right? Maybe even wish him a happy birthday."

She says the words steadily and then turns for home.

Leaving us alone by Alona in her tree form.

"She knew we were sneaking out," Marley says flatly.

"Marley," I prod. "Are you all right?"

He waves away my forced question. "Fine."

"Who was he—"

"No one," he says curtly. "He was nobody, Ramya."

CHAPTER SEVENTEEN

BAD FORTUNE

We fly the dragon to Edinburgh a second time.

"You shouldn't have come back."

Freddy says the words, but I can see a flicker of happiness at the sight of the four of us. Marley, Alona, Blue, and me. Alona has borrowed one of Marley's oversized hoodies, so as to hide her obvious dryad features. Blue is merrily sinking into the River Forth after a long journey from Loch Ness, splashing her tail for her own amusement.

"We won't be long, girl," I tell the huge dragon as she begins to disappear.

She gives me a blink that conveys a lot of disbelief.

"Can I . . . ?" Freddy takes a tentative step toward

the river, staring at Blue. "I've never seen anything like a dragon before."

Blue snarls at first, and it terrifies me, even though it's directed at Freddy. He hesitates but is determined. He stretches out his hand, palm open, and gives Blue her own space to respond. Her snarl softens, but her eyes are fixed upon him with unwavering fierceness. Her nostrils flare, and her tail suddenly twitches.

Freddy stands firm. He lowers his eyes, deliberately unconfrontational.

We all watch and wait. Alona is holding her breath; Marley is glancing between Freddy and the dragon.

I feel calm. I know Blue will see what I see.

She rests her giant chin on top of Freddy's open palm and closes her eyes. It's a docile act, but at no point do any of us forget she is a dragon. I look at Freddy's face, and I'm shocked to see that his eyes are shining.

"She likes you," I tell him, trying to be reassuring.

"Yes," he says, sounding slightly breathless.

I'm confused. "That's good, Freddy. Right?"

"It's just"—he smiles sadly at me and then looks back at the dragon—"Hidden creatures rarely like me. Humans like me a little too much, but other magical creatures . . . they never do. This is just . . . It's nice, is all."

He brings up his other hand to gently touch the dragon's face. It's strangely beautiful. A siren boy and a water dragon, the Loch Ness "Monster" herself, gently touching each other.

For a moment I forget. I forget why we're here, and I just enjoy the peace of it all.

Freddy holds a lot of that peace within himself as we leave Blue and set off into town, the lights of Edinburgh a little brighter than the last time we visited. Curfew has been set to a later time of night, we are told. I watch the humans as they move around the city in eerie contentedness. I'm sure if I asked them, they would be shocked to know that their behavior has become so influenced by one person. A siren.

"There's a Christmas market up now," Freddy tells us.

"How is your mother controlling them all?" I ask him. "Ren wanted to get close to my parents because they were on television. Is that what she's using?"

"Not to my knowledge," Freddy replies. "I think it's radio."

"Radio?" Marley and I say in unison.

"Yeah," Freddy says, nodding. "She does one broadcast a day. Plus, the entire parliament is in her thrall. And the council."

"I still can't believe you forgot to mention you're

her son," Marley mutters. "Nothing dodgy about that at all."

Freddy throws him a sly look. "Trip on that curb."

Milliseconds after he says it, Marley does. Compelled to. He shakes himself brutally and looks angry enough to strike Freddy.

"Don't do that," I tell Freddy softly. "He's had enough sirens for a lifetime."

Freddy is suitably chastised and leaves Marley alone for the rest of our walk into town. The city is almost as I remember it, aglow with the artificial lights of a bustling town beneath bright stars in a clear sky. It, for a brief and flickering second, almost feels like home again.

"Where could your mum be keeping him?" I ask, turning to Freddy and speaking low. "Not at your house."

"No," he agrees. "I checked out the parliament building and the palace, but there's nothing there. She would need somewhere with a lot of space, and she's always had a weakness for grandeur. So maybe the castle?"

We all gaze up, beyond the Scott Monument, to the stone castle sitting upon the high hilltop overlooking the entire city, both New Town and Old.

"It's a fortress," Alona concedes. "It would be a smart choice."

"We could break in," I say. "But probably not out."

"I just need to see he's alive," she says brokenly. "That's all I want for tonight; I'll take that much."

I feel the same about Murrey. Except I'm determined to rescue him and any other Hidden Folk she has chained up.

"Remember, she wants you to find her," Freddy tells me. "Don't be rash. Don't be impulsive."

"Me? Rash and impulsive?" I turn to grin at him, and he can't help smiling back. He nudges me, and I dig my elbow into his ribs.

"Are they always . . . like this?" Alona asks Marley in a stage whisper.

"Yes," he says stonily. "It's revolting."

I spot the Christmas market on the other side of the large Gothic monument before us. I head toward it, recognizing the stalls as Edinburgh's usual vendors. Aboveground, human vendors, that is. Sweets, candy floss, and hot dog stands with the occasional jewelry merchant—all is as it usually is.

Apart from one caravan.

It is teal in color and new to the Christmas market. A sign outside says:

Madame Lylah's Parlor: Fortunes Told Inside

"Ramya," Marley says. "A real fortune teller?"

"Hard to say," I reply. "In the books Opal had me read, there were passages about some witches who have clairvoyance, and a few Druids. It's possible."

"Let's see. She could be Hidden and know some answers."

I nod, and we head toward Madame Lylah's little home on wheels. "You two stand guard," I tell Freddy and Alona.

"Don't leave me with the siren," she says, eyeing Freddy.

"Alona." I say her name gently. "Freddy is my friend. I trust him. Just the same as you are my friend and I trust you. So you can trust each other."

She lowers her eyes and glances away, almost embarrassed. I frown. It was not the reaction I wanted. I was trying to reassure her.

"Wait here and stay safe," I reiterate. "We'll check this out."

We enter the caravan, and as soon as the curtain falls behind us, all outdoor noise vanishes. The light inside is dim, with only a few candles burning. Sitting in a chair, in the farthest corner of the small wagon, is a woman with silver hair and aquamarine eyes. She looks up sharply as we enter.

"We need answers about some friends of ours," I tell her, wondering if we're meeting a genuine fortune teller or a charlatan. "We need to find them."

She considers me. Then nods toward a small side

table with a magenta cloth tossed over it. There is no crystal ball, just a rose. For a moment, something about the single stem makes me forget why we've come. I stare at the satin petals and feel very calm.

"Sit," she says firmly, and we do.

She takes my hand immediately and begins to examine it. "You are lost."

I find my eyes wandering lazily to the rose, but I force them back to Madame Lylah. "No. My friends are. Murrey and—"

"You," she repeats, "are lost. You are forgetting who you are."

I look back at the flower. "What is that?"

She looks too. Then back at me, with a glaze of cunning in her face. "What if I told you every petal grants you a wish?"

"Ramya," Marley says nervously.

I stare her right in the eye. "Then I wouldn't believe you."

She wheezes, and I notice lines around her eyes. "Clever witch."

Her finger is still stroking the palm of my hand, and I feel sleepy at the touch.

"Where are my friends?" I echo, the words a chant I need to recite when I begin to forget why we've come here.

"Can you be sure they are your friends?" she

challenges. "You say you trust your friends, but they hope to betray you."

Freddy. The words sting, but I ignore them. "That's a lie."

"It is not. It is currently a fleeting thought, but we will see."

"Where is Murrey?" I push. I have to physically force myself to stop looking at the rose. "And what spell is in that flower?"

"Just a soothing charm," she says, still hypnotically stroking my hand. "You once stole two pounds."

I freeze. "What did you say?"

"You used it to buy a pen everyone else in the class already had. But you threw it out when your handwriting remained unchanged."

"How . . . how could you know—"

"It's all here. In your hands."

The hands in question begin to sweat, and I have to shiver myself into remembering my mantra. "Where are my friends?"

"The Druid is not your friend."

"The vampire is."

"Yes."

"So where is he?"

"Dying."

I let out a cry and make to snatch my hand away, but she holds on even more tightly. "No!"

"I see a cell. And the siren. She wants to know what is keeping him alive. She cannot understand it."

"Please." There is a crack in my voice. "I have to find him. He's innocent. He's a good person. He would never hurt anyone. Please."

She regards me, her eyes casually flitting to Marley. "You are not ready for her."

"I am," I say doggedly. "I am, I'm ready. I just need to know where she's keeping him."

Her eyes flash, and she suddenly releases my hand. I jerk back and hold it close to my body.

"They are being kept beneath the throne of the last great king," she finally says. "Through a hidden door, down a narrow path, and deep in the heart. There they will be."

I stare at her, then turn to Marley. He seems as baffled as I feel, but then I see a glimmer of understanding cross his face and I am instantly alert. "Let's go," I tell him. "Now."

We're rushing to leave when Lylah calls, "Boy?" Marley turns, his expression hesitant.

"Your mother knew you ran away when you were ten," she whispers, gazing up at him. "She forgave you when you came back. Pretended not to notice. But she thinks about it. Every night."

I frown and look at my cousin. I'm unnerved to find all the color gone from his face. He shoves his way out of the wagon and is gone, leaving me alone with this cryptic, somewhat frightening woman.

"Tick-tock, little witch," she warns. "And watch yourself on the stairs."

CHAPTER EIGHTEEN

SILVER

Alona is seething as we ready ourselves to fly back to Loch Ness. I'm in agreement with her. I was willing to force the answer to the riddle out of Marley and go after Murrey and the Druid there and then, but Freddy told us that plan would surely get us all captured, and then he herded us out of the market. Fae were showing up with bells, letting everyone know that curfew would soon be in place. We had to return to Blue, but I wasn't going to waste a moment.

"We rest tomorrow. Then we plan. And then we go." Alona seems settled by my words. Marley says nothing.

"Freddy." I lean down as Blue is about to take off.

My siren friend glances up at the three of us. "Come with us. Who knows if it's safe for you here."

He hesitates. "Doesn't really sound like a siren is welcome at Loch Ness."

"They're not," mutters Alona.

"You are," I tell him emphatically. "You're my friend. You're welcome."

For a moment, it looks as if he might say yes. "I have work to do here. I need to be there to help Erica and the Hidden Folk. They need supplies, the ones who are hiding."

I nod in understanding. "Okay. But we'll be back. Soon."

He reaches up to squeeze my wrist. "You're not wearing your beret."

"Oh." I'm jarred by his words. "I forgot to put it on. I've been . . . busy."

Blue chooses that moment to fly. She takes off, and I'm still staring down at Freddy until he is out of sight.

I hadn't even realized my beret was gone.

I can feel both Alona and Marley peering at me throughout the flight, but I say nothing. I suddenly realize how tired I am. Days of irregular sleep because of our sneaking out have crept up on me. As Blue begins her descent into Loch Ness, I can picture my bed in the tower, and I can't wait to crawl into it and pretend that none of this is really happening.

"Ramya!" shrieks Alona, jolting me out of my reverie. She's pointing to the bank of the loch as Blue begins to land upon the water. "It's him!"

Marley and I instantly grab hold of the dryad before she can splash through the cold water toward what appears to be her maker upon the dry land.

"It's not him," I tell her, hugging her from behind. "Wait. Watch."

I can feel her desperation to run to the doppelgänger, but she obeys me. She stills, and we all watch the man on the bank. He stares back for a moment and then transforms. Into Aunt Opal, then Aunt Leanna, then me. I grimace and let go of Alona.

"See. It's a weird shape-shifter."

"And this is what Portia wants?" she whispers, gaping at it. "This is the ghost everyone has been seeing. That's what she wants?"

"She's collecting powerful Hidden Folk for her personal guard," I say, sighing.

"It was just like him," Alona breathes. "Now it looks just like you."

I stare into my own eyes, and then the creature shifts once more. As if it has somehow scanned my brain, my memory, it turns into Mum. I clench my fists.

Then it turns into Grandpa.

The snarl that comes out of my mouth feels

animalistic. No one is strong enough to hold me back as I reach down for a stone and hurl it.

"Don't you dare wear his face!" I scream, throwing another. The shape-shifter does not even flinch. Instead, it throws the stones back. They miss me, but the retaliation makes me even more furious. I blast some magic toward it. A spell hits it directly in the face and it staggers backward a little.

"Ramya, stop," Marley says.

I reach down to pick up another stone, but my weak ankles lose their footing and I collapse onto the ground. I swear and can feel spluttering, angry sobs threatening to break loose.

So I let them out. The creature vanishes at the sound, and Blue, still standing in the water behind us, gives a low moan.

"I hate this," I choke out. "I hate feeling useless."

"You're not useless," Alona says gently. "Your magic is the reason the fae and Portia are afraid to seize you. You're lucky."

"I don't feel lucky. They've locked up my friend to get to me. They know that every minute I'm not trying to break him out, I'm feeling guilty. Knowing that he's in there because they're trying to lure me out."

I punch the stones and dirt beneath my tightly closed fists. I punch until it hurts.

"You'll injure yourself," Alona says, kneeling next

to me. She holds one of my hands and steadies it. I can't look at her; I feel like an electric wire that has sparked too brightly.

"We need to plan a rescue. Now." I turn to Marley. "What did that fortune teller mean? The king's throne. What is that?"

Marley casts a glance at where the creature stood and then considers the question. "I was thinking about that as we were flying back. Maybe Arthur's Seat?"

Arthur's Seat, the dormant volcano overlooking the city. Now a popular sight for tourists, hillwalkers, and school geology trips. I frown.

"Arthur's Seat got its name because people believe that to be where Camelot stood. It makes sense with the riddle."

"Agreed," I concede, "but it's outdoors. Why would her hideout be on top of a hill?"

"She said something about a secret door and a narrow path," Marley reminds me.

"She did," I murmur. I glance at him. "You really think—"

"I do," he says soundly. "But the door will be Glamoured."

"Yes. So when do we—"

"Daylight," Marley says, and I'm surprised by how resolute he sounds. "Tomorrow, we have to just go. If Mum or Aunt Opal tries to stop us—"

“They won’t if we slip out before dinner,” I point out. “We’ll be on Blue and gone before they notice.”

“Aunt Opal knows we’ve been—”

“She doesn’t know everything, and she doesn’t know about Blue.”

“I’ll be in our cottage,” Alona tells us. “I have to . . . I have to tidy it up, for when he gets back. Knock on the door. I’ll come with you. I want to help.”

“You don’t want to stay by our house?” I ask.

“Oh, no,” she says hurriedly. “It’s all right. I want to be home.”

We watch her scamper away, and when she is almost out of sight, she transforms into a leaf and floats across the breeze. We sit in silence for a moment, my cheeks damp with frustrated tears.

“I want to go home too,” I say, and he knows I mean Edinburgh.

“I know.”

“Marley?”

“Yes?”

“I . . .” I feel another sob lodged in my throat, and I have to squeeze my eyes closed to hold back more tears. “I really do try, you know. I’m really trying.”

I feel his hand on my shoulder. “I know you are.”

When I flew for the first time, so long ago now, with Aunt Opal and the kelpies and the river beneath me, I thought I was finally a natural at something. I thought a talent had finally come easy to me, that I would finally be able to do something without constant practice.

The more I've allowed doubt to set in, the harder it has been to fly. I've told myself that my wings have been clipped, but in reality, I'm just too afraid to use them.

*

"AUNT OPAL?"

It's noon the next day and she's in Grandpa's study. I knock on the door and poke my head in. She's sitting cross-legged on top of his old writing desk, reading something. She glances up when I enter and smiles lightly. "Hey."

"What's that?" I ask, nodding at the book in her hands.

She looks down at it once more, and her eyes soften. "One of Dad's first attempts at a book on the Hidden Folk."

I move a little closer. "He always wished he could see them."

"Yeah, well." She turns a page. "They mostly grew to like him so much that they would let down their Glamour on occasion. Not all of them, but some."

"He was the best."

"Yeah. But he could push. When he wanted results, when he had a vision in his head, he could overwork himself. And other people."

I blink, unsure of how to respond. "He could?"

"Yes. Why do you think your mum works so hard? Why do you think Aunt Leanna is so worried about Marley? And me. I'm . . . well. Me."

"You push me hard," I point out, not unkindly.

"I do. Because I know you can do better."

I don't know how to tell her that a compliment would make me work fifty times harder. I can't express in this moment how much I need to feel like I'm doing well, in order to do better. I'm tired of playing the underdog. I'm tired of feeling like I have to fight my way out of every room and every situation. "Okay."

We sit together in the dusty, bookish room without making a sound. I view the photographs on Grandpa's wall.

I spot one that seems like me. One year old, sitting on the kitchen floor with a plastic toy telephone. My pudgy little hand is holding the phone up to Aunt Opal, and she is pretending to listen in to an imaginary caller on the other end. I'm looking up at her and laughing. Gran and Grandpa are in the background, smiling as well.

I stare at it. "I didn't . . . I didn't know you were there. In the beginning."

She examines the photograph, and a flicker of emotion streaks through her eyes, then vanishes. "Of course I was."

I turn to another photograph. This one only of her. She's wearing faded jeans and a crop top, smiling knowingly at the camera.

"My best friend took that one," she says quietly. "Funny to look at it now."

I'm about to ask who she's referring to when she sniffs and points out the study window. "That dryad. She's your friend?"

"Yes," I say firmly. "She's sweet. You'd like her if you met her on a normal day. You know, one where her maker hasn't been kidnapped by a siren."

Opal laughs bitterly. "I'm sure I would."

"She's never had friends before us."

"And she's who you've been sneaking out to see?"

I feel color rush to my neck, and I blush furiously. "Yes."

I say nothing of Blue, the dragon.

"Okay. As long as you're keeping to the house and are safe."

"We are," I lie.

"Good friends are . . . more precious than anything," she adds, turning back to the single photograph of her when she was younger. "Don't let them become living ghosts in your life. Or faces you can't really remember."

I can see how tired she is. "Why are you conserving your magic?"

She touches the satin teal fabric around her wrist, the one the Stranger gifted her. "I'm working on one very big spell."

"A curse?"

"Maybe."

"Can I know?"

"No."

I want to object but don't let my temper loose. "That shape-shifting thing was like Grandpa. I hate it."

"Leave that thing be."

"Why should I? It's provoking us."

"Ramya."

"What does Portia want with it? Will it do what she says?"

"Remember when I told you to lay low in Edinburgh?" Opal suddenly says. "I told you what you were doing was dangerous. Not to do it."

"You didn't know about Ren."

"No, I didn't. I knew a siren was in town, but I didn't know it was him, you're right. I didn't know Ren. He was ambitious. He was cruel. He wanted power."

"Same as Portia."

"No," Opal breathes, so quietly. "She wants something else. And the best thing you can do is stay here. Not let her get it."

"Me?"

She looks up at me. "Not exactly."

"She wants me because I'm sort of like the chosen one. You know? I have lots of potential and power."

Something is stirring in Opal's face. "You do. But that's not—"

"Dinnertime in twenty minutes!" Aunt Leanna's voice booms from the kitchen, across the hall from the study.

I turn back to Opal. "What were you going to say?"

She shakes her head slightly and smiles. "Nothing."

I wait to see if she will say anything more, but she returns her attention to the book in her lap, only after casting one last glance at the photo on the wall. I am dismissed, once again. I creep out of the room, shutting the door behind me. I spot Marley on the staircase. He nods at me, a questioning gleam in his eye. I nod back.

This is it. We're leaving. To save Murrey, reunite Alona and her maker, and take on the siren.

Marley looks to the kitchen door, I to the study. Then we quietly sneak out the front door together.

★

WE ARE BOTH PANTING AS we sprint to the cottage. I whistle as softly as I can, a warning for Blue. We reach the door and I don't bother to knock, flinging it open.

"Now or never, Alona," I say as I enter with a flourish. "We're leaving now, are you . . ."

My words fade away. The cottage is spick-and-span once again, but completely silent. I check each room, calling her name, but there is no sign of her.

"Ramya?"

I return to the hearth at the sound of Marley calling my name. "She's not here."

"Here," he says, holding up a piece of parchment. It's as white as his face.

A little dryad and a vampire, sharing a cell. He hasn't had any blood in weeks. Hope she is feeling brave. See you shortly, little witch.

My hands shake as I read the words. The swirling, vain penmanship screams fae. Or Portia. I don't even care. I'm enraged, and my skin is hot. I crumple up the piece of paper and hurl it at the stone wall.

"They've got her," Marley says dolefully. "They must have come last night, or this morning—"

"Doesn't matter," I snarl, kicking the door open and heading for the loch, knowing Marley will follow. "We're rescuing three people now instead of two, so what. Plan is the same. We haven't got time to spare anymore."

"They've been starving Murrey," Marley points out as we rush to the water's edge. "That's not only cruel, it's dangerous. He's a vampire. He might—"

"I know, Marley," I snap. "I know."

The evening light is dim as we reach the edge of the loch. I whistle again, and I can see a dark shape coming closer, beneath the water. Blue rises up, and I am momentarily distracted from rage and fear as I marvel at how glorious she really is.

"Up for one more Edinburgh journey, girl?" I ask, touching her snout gently.

She chuffs, and Marley mounts up. I hesitate, staring back over at the cottage, now shrouded in darkness.

Something is not right. Among everything else in this moment, where all seems out of place and impossible to fix, something in the shadows sets off a shiver in me.

"Hello?"

A shape materializes out of the gloom. Alona.

Something is badly wrong. I whisper for Blue to stay away, then turn to address Marley. "I'll go alone. You stay here with Blue."

"Are you mad?"

"Always. But just do it, okay?"

Before he can protest, I move. I walk slowly

toward what looks exactly like my friend, with green eyelashes and a kind, open face. I try to appear unassuming.

"Alona?"

The creature silently stares back.

"You're not her, are you?" I say wearily, edging a little closer. "You're that thing."

She says nothing. Then she transforms. Marley is suddenly standing before me.

I seethe. "What do you do, then? Do you steal our memories? Push your way into our minds? You're disgusting."

"Oh, Ramya, that's so mean."

Another voice speaks, stealing my attention from the frightening creature. Its eyes look over my head, and I know someone else is behind me.

I don't look, I just react. Blasting a flash of magic in the direction of the voice. The shape in the dark corner by the cottage wall deflects the spell, and I gape in horror as Alona's Druid moves into the low light.

"You. You're with Portia."

I'm not even surprised. I never liked him; he was strange from the beginning. But my mind is too focused on my friends to care about this clown right at this moment. A small voice whispers about how Opal clearly suspected this. That was why she felt no urgency to rescue the Druid.

"You've been working for her," I say. My aunt knew it. I should've known it.

"Not in the beginning," he says, shrugging. "But I'm old and worn out. I want to be on the winning side, whatever that is. And a siren who has taken over a whole city while the coven of witches cower up north? That's the side I must be on, I'm afraid."

"Alona trusted you."

"She's too emotional," he sighs. "She'll learn."

I blast another spell, and this one hits him. He stumbles but remains standing, glaring at me.

"I don't want to hurt you," I say sullenly. "Even now. You're just in my way."

"Portia wants to wait for you to come to her, but I'd rather bring you in myself. This creature too. That's what I came for. You're a nice little added bonus. Then she'll—"

"Then she'll respect you for the creepy, brown-nosing minion that you are? Good luck with that. You're not taking me anywhere."

I turn around, prepared to go back to Marley and Blue. My gait is clumsy and jerky.

I hear the Druid tell the strange creature, "Stop her."

I feel and hear the shape-shifter chase me, before my waist is seized and I'm jerked backward.

CHAPTER NINETEEN

REFLECTION

I yelp as we grapple. The more I struggle, the more it fights, and I cannot stabilize myself enough to use my magic. I kick out at the thing, but it's able to stand its ground more gracefully than I can.

"Hold her there," the Druid says casually, and the creature obeys.

It wraps around me from behind like a strait-jacket, and I can't see if it's still wearing my face. "Portia wants me alive."

"I suppose."

Blue suddenly roars. It's a frightening sound—even I flinch. The Druid gasps, seeing her properly for the first time. She charges, and he throws up some kind of enchanted shield, locking me, himself, and the creature inside a protected dome.

"Why did you make it seem like they kidnapped you?" I demand.

"They never came for me—I joined them voluntarily," he admits, his eyes scanning the dome he has made, checking it for flaws. I suppose the fear of a dragon is a good motivator for casting a secure charm.

"What is this thing?" I force out through a clenched jaw, still struggling against the strange shape-shifter.

"Quite a fascinating creature, isn't it?" says the Druid, and his tone is genuine. He moves nearer to us. "It seems eager to obey, and it can transform its own image to mirror the appearances of others. Or their memories. It really is a potential weapon. I can see why Portia wants it. It's from a neighboring loch, must have swum to this one. Clever. She calls it the Ripple."

"I don't care what she calls anything," I say bitterly. I turn to Marley and Blue. I wave my arms frantically, signaling for them to leave. I see Blue snort, and Marley shakes his head determinedly. I continue to gesticulate.

"Go," I say hoarsely, my throat like sand. "Get out of here!"

Marley's face hardens in resolve. He jumps down from Blue and starts to run, around our strange dome and in the direction of the house.

I'm relieved and terrified.

"Portia wants me for her council," I say, rounding on the Druid. "They've captured Alona. Don't you feel guilty?"

"They won't hurt her," he says, shrugging. "They'll return her safely if I hand you over. And this thing, they want it more than anything."

"It's a thug," I snarl. "Why can't we fight fair? You scared of a girl?"

He smirks. "I think you overestimate your abilities. You're good at antagonizing people, I give you that. But how much work do you actually put into your craft?"

"Order this creepy thing to let me go and you can see," I say, deceptively calm.

He considers me, doubt flashing in his eyes for a microsecond. "Release her."

The Ripple obeys, and I exhale a whoosh of sound as my arms are suddenly free. I fall forward and take too long to get my balance; the Druid has already raised his arms. While the shielded dome remains, he has enough skill to prepare a hex. I rush myself through the internal preparation, but I can only manage a defensive jinx, one that knocks his spell to the side.

"If that's the best you can do, I'm not worried." He laughs darkly. "I think you overestimate your importance."

I glare up at him. "No. I am important."

I use both hands to blast a hex toward him, and I feel the energy sag out of me as I do. It's alarming.

He is merely toying with me; I'm not strong enough to defeat him. The sinking realization hits me. I try to call to the water, my best element, but the shield is too strong.

I deflect some of his spells, but he throws more at me so casually, until my knees give in and I'm on my side.

"This is just sad," he says, sighing. "Had enough? I'll take you to Portia if so."

I'm breathing unevenly, and my whole body aches, muscles that are not used to being employed protesting in pain. I cast one last feeble attempt at a hex, and it falls flat, landing on the grass before his feet like a faulty sparkler.

I feel the pressure in my head tightening, and the agony drowns out his derisive laughter. Then I feel the ground rumble. A flash of bright light. Through blurry vision I see the Druid fall backward, his laughter instantly gone. The shield falls apart all around us, his concentration shattered. I blink against the pain and see a pair of kitten heels land neatly on the ground in front of me. I feel the urge to giggle, the sight is so funny to me for some reason.

Her voice is clear to my ears, despite my disorientation.

Opal is now the only shield I see, and her hands crackle with the fibers of magic as she stares down the Druid.

"Get away from my kid."

The Druid is panting. He throws a spell, but she bounces it back like she's playing tennis. She throws one of her own, and a fierce gash appears on the man's cheek.

"Turn the other way, I'll make it symmetrical," she snaps.

The Druid is momentarily distracted, crying out as he touches the wound on his face. Opal hauls me to my feet and pushes me toward the water.

"Please tell me that dragon likes you," she utters, and I bark out a hysterical laugh.

"I'm sorry, Opal," I gasp, my voice sounding strange to me. "I'm so sorry."

"Get to the dragon, babe," she says breathlessly. "Go. I've got him, go. Get out of this place."

I hate myself in this moment. We had a house protected by magic. And I made every attempt to escape it. I squandered it. I messed everything up, and now Aunt Opal has to clean up after me.

I watch them duel as I crawl toward Blue. I hope Marley is with Aunt Leanna. In our safe, warm home. I hope we'll all be seated around the dinner table, being told off, in an hour.

I've never wanted to be scolded before, but now it sounds like bliss.

"Kill her!" the Druid instructs the Ripple, pointing at Aunt Opal. The creature is confused. I crane my neck and watch as Opal's eyes land on the thing. It transforms into Mum and then Aunt Leanna.

Opal curses aloud and blasts one final spell at the Druid. It floors him once again, and she takes her opportunity to run to me. I can tell she is still sparing her magic, conserving her energy for this mysterious assignment she has given herself. She grabs me by the waist, and we are airborne.

It is slow and heavy, especially as she concentrates on holding on to me. I'm too weak to fly myself, too weak to help her. She glances down once more—we both do—and I feel her whole body go stiff.

The Ripple has turned into Grandpa again. It stares up at the two of us, wearing his face. I hear Opal make a noise of pain, and everything slows down for me. I know she's trying to get us out, holding back on her magic to focus on flying, but the Druid is not. I watch as he launches one final spell. It's maroon in color, like blood that smells of iron, and I watch it hit Opal in the ribs. I wonder if I have imagined it, because she does not react at first. Her face is smooth and peaceful. Then I feel her grip on me loosen. I must be screaming, I can sense it, but I can't hear it.

We lock eyes, and for a split second, I think everything might just be all right, as she fights to smile, trying desperately to be encouraging. I feel myself mirroring her expression, her attempts to assure me that it will all come right.

"It's fine," I say brokenly, smiling while a tear drops into the air beneath us. "You're fine."

Her eyes continue to try to hold mine, but something in them is fading. Her smile, already so weak, loses the last of its strength.

Then she lets go.

Her fingers release my waist, and I know I must be falling too, but I still can't feel it. I am frozen in time as I watch her descend. She closes her eyes right before landing on the hard ground, and a few seconds later, my knees hit the grass and the stones as well. I struggle toward her.

"I'll get Aunt Leanna," I tell her, my words barely in order—my ability to speak more muddled than ever. I grasp her cold hand and squeeze it, probably too hard. "She'll—she'll fix this. She'll fix you. You don't need fixing. Sorry. I m-meant she'll make it hurt less. I bet it hurts. But it's—it's going to be fine."

There is not a flicker of life in her, not a single inch of movement to make me think she can hear or sense me. She is not breathing. I am somehow aware of the Druid casting another shield around us, while screaming at Blue to stay back. I can make out Blue roaring, but it sounds like an echo from the other side of a great cave. I feel the Ripple watching us.

"It's fine," I tell Opal again, rubbing her hand to try to warm it. "I just need you to stay here now."

I don't even know what I'm saying. What mantra I am repeating over and over again, using home and her face like a charm. I use every word I know in the desperate belief that it might craft together some spell that will fix all of this, undo all the terrible decisions I've made and save my family, whom I've put in danger with my impulsiveness. I use all the magic I have, hoping to bring everything back to how it was yesterday. Yesterday, when I thought everything was so bleak, not realizing that so much good was there, right there.

"Somebody HELP ME!" I yell, my words bouncing off the shield. "ANYBODY! PLEASE!"

I feel myself being pulled away from Opal, and my screams turn to feral snarls and then wailing cries.

"I just want to be with my family," I say, uttering it over and over to myself like a prayer while pulling on her limp hand. "I just want to be with my family. I just want to be with my family."

I feel a pinch, and everything falls away into darkness.

CHAPTER TWENTY

CAMELOT

I wake up somewhere damp and chilled and shut away from any natural light. A dim candle is lit, but it takes a few blinks and sitting up before my eyes focus on my surroundings. Someone is kneeling in front of me, sitting back on their heels as if they are examining me.

When I recognize who it is, I lunge forward. Only to find that I have a chain around my wrist, attached to the stone wall behind me.

"Finally awake," Portia says blandly. "You had me a bit worried."

I pull feebly on my chain and realize that I'm trapped in some kind of underground cell. "Is this Arthur's Seat?"

My voice sounds as if I have been drinking seawater.

"Sure is," Portia says chirpily. "I know a hideout inside an old volcano is a bit passé, but I'm a traditionalist. I thought you'd make your own way here when we took your little woodland friend, but ho hum. The Druid dropping you off is fine, too, I guess. Not quite as poetic."

"Where's Alona—what have you done with her?"

"I'm here, Ramya," a tiny, quiet voice says, and I see her behind Portia, sitting curled up in another corner of the cell. She is watching me with fear, as if I'm the deadly siren.

"You okay?" I wheeze. "We were on our way."

"I'm fine," she says, avoiding my eye. "You—you shouldn't have come."

"Do you maybe want to tell Ramya why that is?" Portia asks, casting a glance back toward the dryad.

"Please don't," she says softly, and her eyes are hitting every centimeter of our cell, but they never land on me. "Please."

"See, Ramya," Portia says genially, "young Alona hasn't been entirely truthful with you. She's not quite the sweet little tree girl you thought she was. She's been doing me a solid and keeping tabs on you for a while, feeding information back to me here while you were both up north."

I don't know how much more I can take. I put a hand to the back of my head, expecting to find a wound. I feel cut into pieces, and I don't think I can hold myself together any longer.

I see Opal's face in my mind, and I suddenly realize I have two ghosts to contend with now.

"Is that true?" I say with poison, glaring at Alona.

She finally looks at me, and she doesn't need to say anything. I can see the guilt and the shame written across her face, little marks of betrayal. I shake my head and let it drop against the wet stone.

"I lost everything to try to rescue someone who doesn't deserve it," I say faintly.

"Shame the Druid couldn't bring that dragon," Portia says thoughtfully. "I could always use one of those. No matter."

"So now what?" I say. "You kill me?"

"Ramya, we've talked about this. Stop being so melodramatic."

"Apologies," I snap. "You've got me locked up in a dungeon, inside an ancient volcano, so I thought we were going full throttle on the melodrama."

"She's good, isn't she?" Portia says, turning to Alona, who looks more miserable than anyone I have ever seen. "I wish she would relax a little. She'd be much more fun."

"You're controlling humans via the radio, aren't

you?" I say. "Telling them to be mistrustful of each other, that kind of stuff?"

"That 'stuff' will ensure a safe future for my son and my kind," Portia says, all levity gone from her demeanor. "Stability is not something to joke about. I'll do anything to make sure my son has the future he deserves. And a world that will accommodate it."

"You don't care about Freddy," I counter, my voice flat and emotionless. "Maybe the parts of him you feel are extra pieces of you. But not him. Not really."

Her eyes darken; I can just make them out in the dim light. "You think because my son's a little enamored with you, you know him better than I do?"

"Yes," I rasp. "I do."

"I think this is a sore subject for you," she says after a small pause. "Where is your family? I'm doing all of this, creating this world, for mine. For my son. Where is yours? Are your parents still too wrapped up in their own lives, in their careers, to notice you're missing? Is your grandmother as cold as ever?"

I sniff, shutting off my feelings like an old, rusty tap. I won't let her have my anger. I've cast it at people for so long when I should have been letting it wither and die. It seems sad. I have finally understood the need to control myself, to preserve my peace instead of rising to other people, and the one person who impressed the importance of that upon me is not here to see it.

"Where's your aunt Opal?"

I force myself to stay unaffected as she asks the question. That pain is private, and this siren cannot make me talk, the way she forces others to.

"Come on, Ramya," she says, something unstable entering her voice. "You're not playing the game properly."

I meet her gaze. "I don't want to play with you anymore. Do what you want to do. If people want to let you control them, fine."

"Ramya," Alona breathes, sounding fragile and afraid.

"Don't speak to me," I reply.

"Oh, girls, don't quarrel," Portia laughs. "You see, Ramya? Your little friends, that's what made you feel so superior to everyone. But guess what? Everyone has a price. Hidden Folk, humans, family members. Best friends. Everyone."

She gets to her feet, slapping her knees in the process. She walks to the back of the cell, where a heavy door is tucked into the corner.

"Well, everyone except this one."

I frown, looking over at her. Even though I'm exhausted and using what little strength I do have to conceal my feelings, I'm unable to mask my horror. Huddled in the final darkened corner, appearing almost dead, is a vampire. One who is far thinner and paler than normal.

"Murrey?" I whisper.

"He's been increasingly stubborn," Portia says flatly. "And I don't fully know what's keeping him alive. But here he is. Anyway. There is only one way out of this cell, and it's up the stairs that are in the antechamber, which leads to the throne room. We're all waiting for you there, when you decide you want to be sensible and make some compromises. I would hurry. He won't be able to hold his thirst for much longer."

I raise my head to glower at her, still keeping a lid on everything I'm feeling. I speak softly and delicately. "I would advise killing me, Portia. Because when I get my strength back, when I get my head in order . . . I'm going to kill you."

She regards me coolly. "You keep digging for a bit of spirit, Ramya. Then that might actually sound believable."

She leaves the room and locks us in together. Just the three of us alone in the fading light. I use every ounce of power I have to crawl over to Murrey, ignoring Alona completely.

"Hey, friend," I say quietly, feeling relief at seeing him alive but devastation at how weak he has become. "Sorry I took so long to get here. But I'm here now. It's all okay."

"Ramya," he says, and his voice is barely there. I touch his cheek, and his shaking hand covers my fingers. "I think I . . . I think I am a bit of a mess."

"No, you're great," I lie. It is such a ridiculous fib, we both laugh. Very wearily. "You look more like how I thought vampires really are. Remember?"

"Yes," he says, and his faint laughter becomes a deep cough. I try to hide my worry. "Back in the library."

"Yeah," I whisper.

"Oh." His coughs subside and his face crumples. "I wish I could be back in the library now."

A tear pools and I nod. "Me too, Murrey. I wish we could be back with the books."

"How's your book coming along?" He coughs again. "Lots of Hidden Folk in Loch Ness, I bet."

"Oh." I clutch his hand and stare down at our interlaced fingers. "Lots. Some you wouldn't believe."

He smiles faintly. "I can't wait to read it."

I force myself to find some strength and plaster on a grin, one that simply can't reach my eyes. "Me neither. I hope you like it."

His smile diminishes. "Thing is . . . I don't know if I'll make it out of this place."

"Yes, you will," I reply, completely resolute. "You will. Do you need blood? You can have mine."

"No," he says. "I would never . . . I would die before hurting my friend."

He closes his eyes, and his breathing settles. I check his pulse, and I'm relieved to feel it beating, albeit slowly. He's just resting. I sit back on my heels and exhale.

Still ignoring the traitor in the room.

"Ramya—"

"Don't speak to me. I'm thinking about how me and my friend are going to get out of here."

"I'm so sorry. They said they would hurt us if I didn't do as they said. The fae, they were so—"

"I'm not interested," I say while examining the door. "No. Wait. I'm lying. How long have you been talking to them about us? Since the very beginning? When you pulled Marley out of the loch—"

"Not then," she says, eyes brimming. "When I couldn't find the house anymore . . . recently—"

"Stop, I don't care," I mutter, rolling my eyes. "Your maker is a monster, by the way. He killed my aunt—"

The words are spoken so casually, until a sob bursts free from my throat and I'm doubled over.

I gasp and then shake myself back into trying to pick the lock. "I hate all of this. I hate . . . living through whatever this is. This war she's decided to thrust all of us into."

"Maybe . . . maybe we don't have to get involved," Alona whispers frantically. "She just wants to keep humans in order, maybe—"

"No. She's hurting Hidden Folk so she can go unchallenged. Doing nothing, hiding out, that's basically taking her side. Letting her get away with it. I won't do that."

"You're far braver than I am."

I stop what I'm doing for a second, anger bubbling up, but I force it down. "Yes. I am. I would never do to you what you've done to us."

Opal told me that forgiving people would set me free. Right at this moment, forgiveness does not sit anywhere in my body. My clumsy hands fumble with what I'm trying to do, they slip and scratch, and my speech is slow and unsteady.

If she wants me to forgive anyone, she can come back from wherever she is and tell me so herself. She can give me that withering look and that sarcastic tone and I won't complain.

I just want her here. I want all of her here.

"Opal gave her life," I finally say. I fall away from the door and blink down at my shaking hands. "That's bravery. Putting yourself in front of someone else without thinking. And what did I do? Let myself get kidnapped and dragged here."

I press my fingers against my eyes and try to push out the wet sting.

"This is all my fault. Everything. She just wanted me to stay in one place and get really good. As good as her, like she thought I could be. But I just wanted to fix everything. I never . . . I never actually stopped and thought about if I was the right person to do it. If I had the capacity, if I had the ability."

I glance over at a sleeping Murrey and then back to the door, which seems impossible right at this moment.

Heavy and unyielding.

"I've never succeeded at anything," I murmur bitterly. "Don't know why I thought I could change that. Can't walk in a straight line. Can't throw or catch. Can barely write by hand. Why did I ever have the audacity to think I could make this situation any better?"

My chain is pulling on the back wall; I can't get any closer to the door. I shuffle backward and turn around, lying down and wrapping my arms around myself. I keep my back to Murrey, Alona, and the door, and I try to forget all of it. Portia's war, her growing council, the city of obedient humans outside this underground fortress.

My family. Whom I may never see again.

My friend who is dying, my friend who betrayed me. I shiver and shake until sleep claims me.

CHAPTER TWENTY-ONE

VALOR

I'm woken by the sound and feel of my chain being unlocked. I'm elated at first, wondering if we're being broken out, but it's one of the fae. Oddly, they do not seem as gleeful as I expect them to. They merely unchain me, stand me up, and start walking me out of the cell.

"Where are you taking her?" groans Murrey, trying to rise.

The faerie uses their boot to force the vampire back into a sitting position. "None of your business. Dryad, you come too."

Alona follows us dutifully, and I scowl at her for doing so. I try to pull against the faerie's grip, but they give me a shake, silently advising me against it. They lead us up a narrow staircase, and their speed is not what I would choose for myself. I trip and stumble and curse them under my breath.

"I'm not good with stairs," I finally snipe. "Take it easy."

When we reach the top, we are led into a large underground court. A great hall with an endlessly high ceiling and an expansive floor.

All of this, buried beneath Arthur's Seat. I wonder what Mr. Ishmael would make of it. Not that I will ever see my old teacher again. I also wonder how Portia's spell has affected him.

Portia is sitting in a large chair on some sort of dais in the northern part of the hall. She has the Druid, another gray-looking man, and some fae around her. They are discussing something. The Druid acts as though he wishes to speak, but every time he opens his mouth to do so, someone else cuts him off.

Then I spot Freddy, sitting with his head on his knees on the edge of the little platform. I resist the urge to shout his name.

"Ah, you're up and about," Portia says, peering at me over the files she is reading. "Feeling chipper?"

"Feel like smashing your head in, actually," I say conversationally. "Thanks."

The faerie shoves me, but Portia holds up a delicate hand. "That won't be necessary. She likes to show off how spirited she can be. It's one of her charming little toxic traits."

"I'm not joining your council," I say loudly. "So, like I mentioned. You might as well kill me."

"Ramya!" Freddy interjects, panic emanating from him.

"It's all right, darling," Portia tells him. "I'm not giving her what she wants just yet. She's not fulfilled her use to me."

I frown. "I said, I'm not joining—"

"Why," Portia says slowly, rising to her feet, "would I want an impulsive, green, untrained little witch on my council? What use could your bad temper and shaky hands offer me? Is that why you think I wanted to lure you here?"

I feel very small all of a sudden. "Then why?"

"You're just the little worm on the hook, sweetheart. I'm trying to catch a much bigger fish. You're not even a shadow of the witch I really want."

I realize who she means, and my eyes flash to the Druid. He is confused, like I was, but I can spot the exact moment when understanding hits him. He goes pale, and his eyes begin to dart around the vast space, as if searching for a way out.

And I start laughing. Then the laughter becomes a guffaw. I can feel their bewilderment, but the screeching sound I am making doesn't stop.

"Madam." The gray man next to Portia looks from me to the high ceiling. "It is . . . raining. Inside."

Little droplets of water start to fall and swirl

around the room, creating an elusive indoor cyclone. I can't stop. The water twitches and turns each time I take a breath between laughs.

"All right, I can take a joke!" Portia shouts. "What's so funny?"

Freddy is suddenly at my side, holding my elbow. "You okay?"

"I'm fine," I snort, still hysterical. "It's just . . . no, I can't."

"Careful," Freddy whispers to me. "That guy next to Mum? His name's Malachi. He's a warlock, and completely brutal."

"Oh, Freddy," I gasp between laughs. "I don't care anymore. They can do what they like." I address the Druid, still snorting through my nose. "Do you want to tell them or should I?"

I have to admit that I enjoy the little dollop of power I get back upon seeing his frantic worry about this new information. He clearly was not in Portia's inner circle, and wasn't aware of Opal or her reputation when he . . .

Remembering what he did sobers me, and my laughter dies out.

"You're hoping I'll be bait to draw in my aunt Opal," I say to Portia.

"That is the dream," she replies sardonically, casting a lazy glance around the enormous chamber. "Turn the water off, please. We are underground.

Unless you want to drown or flush out all the Hidden Folk locked away downstairs."

So Murrey is not the only one chained up.

I force myself to settle, picturing things that can ground me, and the water dissipates before vanishing altogether.

"Very good, Ramya," Portia remarks. "You do have a little control, it seems."

The Druid has edged a little nearer to one of the doors, which I take for an exit. I lock that piece of information away. He is deeply uncomfortable and is clearly formulating a plan of escape in his mind.

Alona is behind me, and when I throw a quick glance at her, I can't help but feel sorry for her, just for a fleeting moment.

She seems absolutely destroyed.

I shoot my gaze back to the front of the chamber. I take in Malachi. His eyes are deadened, and he doesn't appear to blink. Warlocks, according to Opal's books, are male witches who lean into darker magic. He certainly looks the part. He is fiddling with what appears to be a coin, and he seems distracted.

"Murrey needs blood, badly," I mutter to Freddy. "He's in the cell they took me from."

I see his eyebrows rise as he processes my words. "I'll see what I can do."

"Freddy, get away from her, please," Portia suddenly calls.

Freddy does not move. The fae glance between him and his mother. The warlock doesn't react, and the Druid edges even nearer to the exit.

"You'll be waiting a very long time for Opal to come," I tell Portia. "Firstly, how would she know that your creepy secret lair is beneath Arthur's Seat?"

"I would have thought that little fortune teller you met told you, and you told your family," Portia says smoothly, and the words chill and disarm me. "Oh, yes, we found her. Hiding in plain sight, quite clever. She's in one of these cells."

I feel anger and indignation rise in me, but once again, I shackle it. "Still. There are other things keeping Opal from coming."

Portia puffs out a sigh and rolls her eyes. "Go on, then. What else?"

My eyes must be shining in the candlelight. I stare straight at the siren. This siren who has heaped so much misery on me and my family, and so much suppression on this incredible town. "She's dead."

Portia's smile slips. "What?"

"She," I whisper, "is dead."

She narrows her eyes at me. "You're lying to buy her time."

I wish that were the truth. "No."

She is utterly still and staring at me as if I have stolen air from her lungs. She turns briefly to Freddy and then back to me.

"What are you talking about?"

I point to the Druid, my blood heating with hatred. "Ask him."

Alona gasps, and Freddy steps closer to me. The fae and the warlock move to look at Alona's maker, while Portia slowly rises to her feet. Every inch of her is quivering with rage, barely contained fury, and it's enough to frighten me, let alone the man on the other end of her fury.

"What is the little witch talking about?" Portia asks the Druid, her voice as calm as Blue's loch but every bit as dangerous. "Would you care to explain to me why you're thinking of running to that door?"

The Druid stumbles forward, and I can hear Alona's panicked breathing behind me.

"Madam." The Druid speaks with thinly veiled terror. "I . . . when I was trying to retrieve the Ripple . . . the other witch attacked me, the elder. She was powerful. And—and there was a dragon!"

"What"—Portia advances on him slowly, like a leopard on its prey—"happened?"

The large room is silent. The only sound is Portia's heels on the ground as she continues her menacing approach. I'm confused by this reaction. There is something missing from my understanding of the situation. Portia is vibrating with rage, that's obvious. That I can understand. Someone has gone rogue and deviated from her plan.

However, there's something else. Her face seems to have a touch of fear in it. I stare at her profile, fascinated by this questionable reaction.

"I killed the witch," the Druid finally admits, and I close my eyes to shut out the memory. "I hit her in the ribs. She fell. She's gone."

At first, there is no reaction at all from Portia. She is completely still and completely silent, her face a mask that I can no longer read. Then suddenly, she reaches out and grabs the Druid's chin. He naturally flinches, but her nails dig into his skin, causing him to freeze and whimper. It is a pathetic sight to witness. The siren roughly jerks his face to the right.

"That cut," she says softly. "That was her?"

He is almost hyperventilating as he nods. "Yes."

I stare in astonishment as Portia reaches out with her other hand to touch the mark, almost a reverent caress.

Then she throws her head back and shrieks, a long and sustained note of anguish that is almost a whistle tone. The fae react with yelps, and Freddy dives to cover my ears. He shields me with his body, and we hit the floor while Portia's scream continues.

When she stops, I look up. The fae are clustered together in a corner, their teeth bared in a hiss. The warlock puts the end of one pinkie finger into his ear and clears out some gunk, shaking his head as if to dislodge echoes of the inhuman sound. Alona is crying quietly behind me.

"Fetch the Ripple," Portia tells the warlock. We all watch him saunter away to do so while Portia's attention never wavers from the Druid.

"I want to cut out your tongue," she murmurs. "You have no idea what you've done."

"I thought you would be pleased," the Druid tries desperately.

"Lock him up with the rest," Portia tells the fae, and they move to carry out the order while the Druid loudly objects.

I expect her to round on us, but she turns to face the wall, hiding her expression from the entire room. Her back and shoulders are stiff, and her breathing is shallow and uneven. The warlock returns with the Ripple. The creature transforms into a plethora of people before settling on doubling as one of the fae.

Portia finally breaks free from her daze and moves toward the strange shape-shifter. While wearing the faerie's face, the creature is afraid. I find myself softening just a touch at the sight. It doesn't seem to know what or who it is underneath the multitude of masks it wears.

As Portia stares at it, it shifts. To the Druid. Then to Freddy.

Then to Opal.

The resemblance is so uncanny, Portia takes a step back, and I have to turn away. It's too painful. I can hear Freddy whispering to me, but I can't process the words.

"You certainly are disconcerting," Portia tells the Ripple, and her voice sounds different. "You'll do just fine."

She seems almost deflated. As if the news, and her resounding reaction, have robbed her of something.

I glance around the massive chamber, taking account of the different doors. Some leading to cells, others perhaps leading nowhere. Behind me, about fifty meters away, are large wooden doors. If Camelot did once exist here, those doors are the only reminder, the only nod to the royal and regal.

I wonder if I can make it to those doors without getting hexed by the warlock or seized by the fae or the Ripple. The idea of running up the steep steps that no doubt await me on the other side is worrying.

I tick over escape plans in my mind, trying to figure out how to get Murrey and myself out of here unharmed. Plus any other Hidden Folk she has chained up.

"So, now what?" I call to the siren. "If this was all an elaborate scheme to lure my aunt here, sorry to disappoint you. One of your henchmen already got rid of her."

I spit the words, my emotions unraveling a little.

I try to imagine that my anger and pain are made of thread and that I have to bind it into twine. I cannot let the whole thing disentangle and fall apart.

"Yes. So I suppose I don't need you anymore."

Portia speaks with such a detached voice, such a flat and empty tone. I blink. Even Freddy and the fae are a little puzzled. She sounds utterly defeated.

She falls into her seat by the wall and gestures limply to Malachi.

The warlock steps forward dutifully, and before I can fully gather myself, he throws a spell at me. I only just dive out of its path.

"Stop!" yells Freddy.

"Restrain my son," Portia tells the fae, staring off into space the entire time.

The Ripple, still looking like Opal, glances around at all of us. Confused and constantly learning, as ever.

"Shift into someone else," Portia tells it, a hint of fury entering her tone. "Now."

While Freddy is dragged to the side, I back up.

Alona watches in horror as Malachi braces to cast again. He is toying with me, completely unbothered by my presence.

He doesn't realize that being underestimated is the key to everything for me.

These last few months, when people have had faith in me, I haven't known what to do. My entire life has been molded and shaped around the knowledge of being discounted. I liked being discounted some of the time. When no one had any expectations, anything that I did was a bonus.

Now? Aunt Opal knew I could do better. She told me all the time.

I didn't know what to do with that.

"You can run—I'll give you a head start," Malachi calls as he builds some fire between his palms.

I didn't know then what to do with Opal's belief. I do now.

I don't need a head start. I do not need to run. I face down this dour gray stranger, and I wait. Everything in me is still and composed. The thread wound neatly, but not too tightly. My feelings are not in a box, they are laced within me. Placed inside me with dignity and privacy because I don't need to show other people my pain for it to count as real.

The blaze is thrown at me, and I release everything. I poise each muscle and ground my feet on the floor.

I cast. No hate or anger in my magic, just like Opal always said.

"I forgive you," I whisper.

And the water comes like an avalanche.

It crashes against the warlock, throwing him into the wall. The fae scream and scatter, releasing Freddy in the process. Everyone is drenched in magic as the blue in the room not only extinguishes the warlock's cast but also covers all else in water and mist.

Only the Ripple approaches me. It wears my face, and then, as if probing my mind for everyone I've ever loved, it flashes through many different appearances. My family, flickering in front of me like a strange dream.

It doesn't move to harm me. It only tries to read me.

I think of the first moment I met this odd creature. When I reached down to throw a stone.

It threw one back. Just as clumsily. Just as weakly.

"You're not a ripple," I say to it quietly. "You're a reflection. You don't do something unless someone does it to you."

This lonely creature, new to the world of magic, only knows how to imitate. And Portia wants to teach it violence and hate.

Its image once again lands on Opal. She must be

so present in my mind, the creature cannot read anything else.

I have no desire to cast stones now. I step forward and hold the shape-shifter, my head against its sternum. It doesn't feel or smell like her, but I want this lonesome oddity to feel something other than fear and loathing.

Though stiff at first, and perhaps deeply bemused, it eventually raises its arms to return the embrace.

It is a moment of peace, one I've been craving, and it calms the final pieces of the storm inside me.

When I gently pull away, the Ripple has shifted once more, and I am looking at myself. Like a strange mirror image, only it doesn't echo my every movement. At least not in real time. I stare into my own face, and I decide to let go. I don't need to retaliate. I don't need to poison myself with dreams of revenge, when I could be living my life and making things better for the people I love.

I always stared at Opal and wondered why she didn't carry more anger around with her, the way I did. I took it for weakness, or rather a lack of fortitude.

I was wasting time with all that red when there was blue to feel. This warm, settled, and strong feeling of magic.

I'm not going to tell myself lies anymore. I'm quite good at magic. But I'm going to get better.

What she always wanted for me.

I shake my hands, stimming out little flecks of magic.

I watch as Malachi rises to a standing position. He starts to charge me, building up to another cast—this one more personal and more intense. The same color as the spell the Druid used on Opal. I brace myself, readying for it.

Until I feel hands on my left shoulder, pushing me. A shove that ejects me from the spell's path. I hit the floor and have only a few seconds to see what has happened.

Alona has physically forced me out of the line of fire and now stands boldly in my place. I scream in protest as Malachi is unable to divert the course of his spell.

It hits Alona in the torso, and her arms spread out like an angel's wings. Her eyes look up, and she begins to transform. Instead of hitting the ground, like Opal, her whole figure cracks and transfigures into a tree. Tall and grand, growing right in the heart of the hall. It is not her usual transformation. This oak tree does not teem with life the way she usually does.

Instead of a body, we have been left with a tree. One that is still and silent and solitary.

"Alona?"

I touch the trunk, my hand hot and wet against the bark. Freddy is running over to us, placing himself between me and the warlock. I hear raised voices, but I don't listen. I don't take in whatever is being said.

I feel what little is left of my heart starting to break.

"Are you happy now, Portia?" I say, running my hands over the roots of the tree, which are now dug deep into the ground. "What else do you want to take from me?"

I force myself to look at her. She still seems disillusioned. None of her infamous gleam is alive in her face anymore. It was something I used to fantasize about. I used to play scenarios in my head, over and over, where the smugly chaotic glint would be wiped out of her eyes.

There is nothing satisfying or glorious about any of this.

"I could never be you," I say softly. "This is hell. If you feel this bad inside, all the time. I could never do it."

Her eyes flit to me, and we stare at each other. "You learn to let it keep you warm."

The words fall between us, and I shake my head. The warlock is in my peripheral vision, too afraid to fire while Freddy stands between us. He awaits another command from Portia, but one does not seem to be forthcoming.

I expect her to speak, but we are all interrupted. We turn to face the large doors at the back of the hall.

Someone is knocking.

CHAPTER TWENTY-TWO

THE SIREN AND THE WITCH

The knock is proud and unapologetic. It gives me hope.

I shakily get to my feet, glancing at Freddy. He gives me a nod of encouragement, and though I don't know what awaits on the other side of the doors, I do know he had some part in it. Portia shifts her stance and clicks her fingers. The fae, a little more reluctantly than usual, gather around her. Malachi sniffs and scowls, eyes pinned to the rear of the room.

"I'm not expecting anyone," Portia says edgily.

I let myself bask in hope for a moment. I let myself dream. "I am."

The doors burst open. A mass of people is revealed,

and I gasp out a breath as I see three women at the front.

My mother, my grandmother, and my aunt Leanna.

Gran stands in the middle of the trio, more glamourous than ever. I can't help but release a snort of laughter as I watch her pointedly and deliberately turn down her hearing aid. Mum splays her hands, and fire flares within her palms. The kind I could only dream of conjuring. Aunt Leanna has her hair scraped back, and before anyone can utter a word, she stretches out both arms and releases green vines.

They twist and turn and slither like emerald snakes across the floor before pinning Malachi and the fae to the wall.

"We surrender!" yells one of the fae, her eyes fixed on Mum's hands and her flames.

"Coward," snarls Portia, taking three steps forward and addressing my family. "I wouldn't advise this, ladies."

My family is backed up by at least fifty Hidden Folk. I see Hulders, Blue Men, selkies, and kelpies. A few sprites hover overhead, and there are even a few fae. They advance into the room, and I watch as Mum glances between the Ripple and me, her face growing confused.

"I'm the real one," I say, pointing to my chest. She

frowns, her eyes drifting to the Ripple. Doubt creeps into her features.

"I still think you all should have done this on day one, if that helps," I add. "Take down Portia, that is."

Mum's expression relaxes, and she sighs irritably. "Yes, it's definitely her."

"This is touching, but a few words from me, and most of you will happily walk yourselves into your cells," Portia says silkily. "In fact—"

She is interrupted by the unimaginably, unmistakably loud drone of bagpipes. I clap a hand over my mouth in delight as my cousin edges to the front of the herd, his face red as he blasts out all his grade-three skills on the ancient and indomitable instrument. Some Hidden Folk drum on anything they can (walls, floors, discarded stone) to add to the cacophony.

"Yes, Marley!" I yell, inwardly taking back every mean thing I ever said about his choice of musical instrument. "Play!"

No one can hear me over the noise. Portia's own fingers move to her ears in distaste. The fae and Malachi are pinned to the wall, and the Ripple has transformed into Marley, as if in admiration. Freddy dashes toward one of the antechambers, and I spot Erica at the front, near Marley. We lock eyes and both break into beams, marveling in relief at the madness of it all.

When Marley runs out of breath, Mum blasts some magic toward Portia, enclosing her in a circle of fire. The siren hisses and steps toward it before checking herself. Her voice has no power over the elements, and she is not immune to burns. She glares at Mum with teeth bared.

Mum shrugs, smirking. "You can't burn this witch, Portia."

I laugh, still strangely delighted. My shoulders sag in relief at the sight of my family, and then I register one absence. Two. Three, when I look to the tree next to me.

Sacrifices that are like ghosts here with us.

I notice lots of other women standing among the Hidden Folk. Some Mum's age, some older. They stare Portia down with as much ferocity as Gran. They must connect to Mum and Gran's mission in some way.

They make an intimidating team, whoever they are.

Then time stands still for me. The room falls quiet, and the large mass of people at the back of the hall parts to create a path.

And a ghost does in fact walk into the room.

Someone makes a noise of disbelief, and I'm not even sure whether it is me. I stare at the figure as they move through the crowd of Hidden Folk to the middle of the hall, stopping before Alona and me.

Opal.

She catches my eye for the briefest moment. She touches her wrist. My eyes drop and note that the teal fabric is still tied there.

"How?" I whisper, but Opal is no longer paying attention to me.

She has to be a ghost. This can't be real. Yet I know if I crawled over and touched her skin, I would feel blood pumping. She is not some ethereal spirit, she is human.

Alive again. Right in front of me.

I expect Portia to take advantage of the silence and use her voice, perhaps to free her only supporters. I watch as Mum makes the fire circle a little calmer. She is watching Portia with acute concentration.

Portia does not seem interested in charming anyone.

She is staring at Opal with the same disbelief that I feel, clearly trying to decipher how this is possible. There is also something I cannot fully name in her face. She is breathing rapidly, and her eyes continue to flit over my aunt with confusion.

Opal looks back, calm and collected. "Hello, Sha."

I gape. The whole room seems to hold a collective breath at the utterance. I stare at the siren, expecting her to hiss or spit at the informal greeting. I expect her to bristle at the impudent smile Opal is wearing.

I expect her to call for her guard, bark orders, and use the full force of her voice to fight back against this new development.

She does none of that. Her smile quivers. As does her voice.

"Hey, you."

The word "you" has a lifetime of stories buried in it, and suddenly things click into place. I cling to the unchanging tree, wishing the dryad who once lived inside it could come back like Aunt Opal and see this bizarre little scene.

Opal's smile becomes sad. None of the frosty bravado she exhibited on Inchkeith is present now. She does not look at this siren the way she did at Ren.

"You always take things too far, Portia," she says, too quietly for people at the back of the great hall to hear. "We're not playing this game anymore."

Aunt Leanna and Gran suddenly set off toward the different antechambers, followed by a handful of Hidden Folk. Leanna's vines continue to bind the fae and the warlock, but Portia does not glance away from Opal. She seems either oblivious to or uncaring of what is going on around her.

"The Druid claims to have killed you."

Opal nods once. "He did."

Portia seems to be as torn about this as I feel. "You always were one for surprises."

"An old friend owed me a favor."

"Speaking of old friends—"

"You know you have to stop all of this, right?" Opal interrupts Portia, her jovial tone edging into a more serious expression. She looks at Portia, and I'm suddenly reminded of the photograph in Grandpa's study. Her face is similar now. They're staring at each other, and there is a connection there that is filled with things the rest of the room will never know. A familiarity that is visible with every movement and gesture. "Let us take the Hidden Folk out of here and you can surrender. Stand trial. We can do this with honor."

Portia laughs shrilly. "Nah, not for me, Opal. That's not going to happen."

I hear a gasp of pain and spin around. Freddy emerges from the cells I was being kept in, his arm slung around an exhausted Murrey. The vampire is leaning against the siren, letting the latter take most of his weight. Not that he could be heavy; he is completely emaciated.

"Freddy," Portia says in a broken little voice. "What are you doing?"

My friend stares at his mother, with a touch of both misery and disgust. "Something I should've done already. Something we're supposed to do."

"You're on their side, then?"

"There are no sides!" shouts Freddy, and the entire hall is gravely silent. His voice, equally powerful as her own, perhaps even more so, echoes and bounces off the stone walls. "You know that, Mum. You create the sides. You draw the line, you make the divide.

"I've racked my brain trying to work out why; I don't understand it. Why you get such pleasure from everyone being at each other's throats, or stuck in a cycle of mindless obedience, I don't know. I'll never know. But not me. It will never be me."

Freddy looks over at the large collective of Hidden Folk, and a decision is made in his eyes.

"Do not obey this woman's instructions if you do not want to," he calls, projecting his voice to the back of the large room. He points to Portia as he speaks. "Do not harm yourselves or your friends for her."

A few whoops of approval meet his pronouncement.

"What a waste," Portia breathes, staring at Freddy. "This won't last, you know. This bright-eyed optimism. Your faith in these lesser beings. What about when that one wants nothing to do with you anymore?"

She jerks her chin toward me. I cling on to Alona and glower at her.

"I don't think," Portia goes on, staring at her son, "you realize how lonely this life is, Freddy. How hard it will be."

Freddy's face is more emotional than I've ever seen

it. "I've already been lonely, Mum. It's all I've ever been. Until now. Now I have friends. And I don't need to order them to like me, they just do. Well"—he glances at my cousin—"sometimes they do."

Marley grins, despite the gravity of everything.

Freddy helps Murrey over to where Erica and some trolls are standing by. They instantly leap into action, helping to tend to the vampire.

"I'm never going to be what you want, Mum," Freddy concludes, glancing back at Portia. "And I'm not sorry for it. I wish you were." He is now standing with his chosen side.

As we all stare at one another, Aunt Leanna calls out to the Hidden Folk. "Do as we discussed: Empty the cells. Set everyone free."

"Bring me the Druid," Opal adds, and Freddy is the one who nods and sets to it. Malachi grimaces against his bindings, and some of the fae who are on our side step forward.

"We will punish our own accordingly," one says, his face as earnest as a member of the fae's can be. "We swear it."

Opal looks to Gran, who nods. Then Opal does too.

The fae pull their own kind free from their traps and walk out, trying to appear dignified. I watch their backs, never fully relaxed.

"There's a dragon outside," Aunt Opal says coolly,

just before they are gone from sight. "So don't try anything funny."

Her words have the intended effect. They fearfully submit and then are gone. Hidden Folk disperse into all the antechambers to fetch their comrades and set them free. Portia still stares at Opal, as if she cannot believe she is there.

"Let's speak, just us two?" she finally volunteers.

Opal shakes her head gently. "No, Sha. You've had plenty of time to speak. This mess, everything you've done to this city, it's done all the speaking for you."

Portia's eyes are glistening, and her voice catches as she responds. "You know . . . all I ever did, everything I ever did, it was just to make you look."

I can feel my jaw slipping open. Aunt Opal does not visibly react. "I've prepared something for you. If you're not willing to surrender."

"No!" Portia cries, slamming her foot against the ground as she staggers closer. "This isn't how it's meant to go. You—you wouldn't do this to an old friend, Opal. Not when you know I'm right."

"You're not right, Portia. There is no 'right' when it comes to ruining people's lives. Trying to wipe out Hidden Folk. You've gone beyond what I ever thought possible."

"We've always been the same," Portia whispers. She falls to her knees, just as Hidden Folk begin to emerge from the many doors around the hall. They are confused and tired. Leanna and Freddy usher them to safety, leading them out through the large doors. "Opal, we've always been different. They don't accept you any more than they accept me."

Opal moves toward the siren and kneels down in front of her. "Sha, I'm a neurodivergent witch. Do you think for a single second I've ever cared about fitting in?"

I choke out a laugh, and for the briefest second, Opal's eyes meet mine and she winks.

"A scorpion cannot help its sting," Portia says, reaching out to grasp Opal's hand. "You can't kill your oldest friend."

"Oh, Sha." Opal's voice is now the one that shakes a little. "I'm not going to kill you. I've been working on something special, specifically for you."

"Take the Druid and the warlock into custody and remove them from this place!" Mum says to some of the other women with Gran. They obey, using magic to turn Malachi's bindings into handcuffs. They are witches too. I watch in fascination as a large group of middle-aged women march the two men out of the great hall.

"Take the wounded out and start tending to them," Gran adds.

Soon the hall is almost empty. As Freddy and Leanna return, only the rest of my family and Portia remain. I still cling to Alona, mere feet away from my aunt and the siren. Kneeling across from each other. The Ripple hides in the shadows of a corner.

"Little boy." Portia addresses Marley. "Do you want your father back? Do you want your family united again? I bet you do. I can make that happen. He has another family now, a wife and three girls. They live in the rich part of town."

Leanna starts for the siren, but Mum and Gran hold her back. The Ripple steps forward and transfigures into that same man from the beach. The one who made Leanna sad, the one I do not recognize.

It makes sense now.

"I can bring him back, Marley," Portia says desperately. "Would you like that? One word from me, he'll come home again. You'll have a family."

Marley shakes his head and smiles a bittersweet smile. "I have all my family here already. Despite your best efforts."

Gran wraps an arm around him, and Mum presses her fingers against his cheek. Portia's expression hardens, all attempts at pretending to be civil gone. She looks to Mum, and her voice is deep and low; it's her final attempt at influence.

"Come closer, Cass. Come and feel this fire."

Mum takes a few steps forward and then yells, forcing herself to stop. She stands still, glaring back at the siren.

"I'm not your puppet anymore," she finally says, and I feel like crying. I remember that night, so long ago, when Mum and Dad were under Portia's spell.

"Walk through the fire," Portia reiterates.

Her voice is powerful enough to force Mum to stumble closer. Until Opal steps in front of her. The two witches, the two sisters, look at each other, and Portia's orders fade. The siren lets out a wretched gasp of fury and then one small and bitter laugh.

"What are you going to do to me?" she finally mutters.

HAMARTIA

Many years ago . . .

Opal was expelled. It was decreed. There was no undoing what had happened, and she wasn't even sure if the truth of the matter would reach her parents. She had taken credit for the fire, knowing Cassandra was still battling with the knowledge of having powers. She was barely able to face the consequences of having them at all.

Cass wanted the big career. The sparkling future. She needed institutions to like her.

Opal did not.

She had run from the school, straight to the gardens.

Princes Street Gardens. She needed the seclusion and the shade and the anonymity of a crowd. It was easier to disappear when there were lots of people around you, she'd always found.

The gardens were quiet for once. As she entered, the large castle loomed high overhead. She made her way to her usual bench and blanched upon realizing that someone else was happily sitting on it.

It was a girl her own age. She couldn't be more than fifteen. She had beautiful eyes, and she sat with a stillness that reminded Opal of the statues dotted all around Edinburgh. As if she were made of marble.

"Don't stare at me."

The marble girl barked the order with an imperious tone that made Opal scowl. "Excuse me?"

The girl was instantly surprised. As if she had only meant to think the words. She stared back at Opal in amazement, and Opal crossed her arms with a haughty flick of her long hair.

"Say something," the girl on the bench snapped.

Opal smirked, almost amused by this stranger and her even stranger commands.

"Sit," the girl said, and when Opal spluttered at the sheer insult of the demand, the other girl leaped to her feet. She moved toward Opal with wide eyes and an expression of complete disbelief.

"You don't do what I say," she finally said.

"Of course not," Opal spat, looking the other girl

up and down with pointed scorn. "Who are you to be telling me what to do? Telling me to sit like a dog. You seem more like a dog than me, with your poodle hair."

The girl's eyes glinted with hunger. "I'm Portia. Who are you? *What* are you?"

Perhaps it was the events of the day that made Opal do it. Exclusion and banishment from education.

Whatever the reason, she harnessed the Edinburgh wind and charged it toward the odd girl. Portia staggered backward, shocked by the force of the breeze. Then Opal opened her palms to reveal spitting and crackling sparks of electricity.

"I'm a witch," Opal said quietly. "So don't tell me what to do. Not ever."

The other girl's eyes were glued to the embers, and where Opal expected to see fear, all she saw was delight.

"Fascinating," Portia finally breathed. "But witches aren't immune to us . . ."

Opal frowned. "What?"

Before they could continue their strange face-off, a group of tourists rounded the bend and began to pile into the garden. They gushed and cooed at the castle overhead, and their cameras clicked endearingly. Opal was jarred out of the moment and began to make her way back up to Princes Street. Then—

"Destroy your camera."

The words were spoken sweetly, from the mouth of the peculiar girl. Opal turned around in surprise, before her eyes widened in horror as she watched one of the tourists obey. Instantly. Without question. She watched the short man stomp on his own digital camera with intense animosity, as if he loathed the little device he'd been so fond of merely seconds earlier.

Opal felt suddenly afraid. This person was more than she appeared.

"Now get into the fountain."

Portia. She said her name was Portia. Opal watched in dismay as the tourists all obeyed this time. They walked serenely into the massive water fountain, seemingly unbothered by their shoes, socks, and hems growing cold and damp.

"How are you doing that?" Opal asked, rewarding this strange creature with the attention she so obviously craved.

"It's my own kind of magic," Portia replied, not turning away from the entranced tourists. "People always do what I tell them to."

Except me, Opal thought, as the two of them stared at each other. *Everyone except me.*

★

PORTIA WAS VERY POPULAR WITH the rest of the family, Opal observed. Her new acquaintance quickly became a friend of her sisters through charm and gentle compulsion. Leanna always wanted to be adored by everyone, though. She would giggle nervously at Portia's occasionally more cutting remarks. She would try to dress like her. She would hang on every word she said, and Opal often caught her retelling Portia's jokes to other people.

Cassandra was fascinated by her as well. Cass would show off her drive and ambition, treating Portia like an equal and a consultant. Portia would smile indulgently while Opal's older sisters peacocked and simpered. Opal's father was warm and welcoming toward Portia, but he always seemed a little disturbed by her remarks. He was cautious around her, Opal noticed. At first it made her defensive; Portia was *her* new friend, after all. Then it made her curious.

Her father's wariness of Portia prompted Opal to remember their first meeting beneath the shadow of the castle. The flicker of delight in Portia's eyes when she'd told the tourist to smash his property.

There was a name for whatever kind of magic Portia had, but Opal couldn't say it yet. She had her suspicions.

"Opal?"

Her father stood in the living room doorway in their house. Laughter and loud conversation could still be heard from the dining room. Opal nodded at him in acknowledgment, and he took this as an invitation to come in and sit down on the sofa. They stayed in silence for a moment, staring at the fire in the hearth and letting the laughter in the other room echo around the house.

"There's something different about your new friend."

He said the words with care and deference, but Opal still bristled. "Since when did this family care about difference? We're not exactly the girls next door."

"She's not a witch, like the three of you," James pointed out. "And this is why compiling a glossary is so important, because—"

"Dad," Opal snapped, and she hated to do it. The two of them were very close, and they never raised their voices to each other, but the youngest witch in the family had grown tired of his obsessive need to categorize all the Hidden Folk. "Enough about your book. I don't know what she is."

Siren. The word was already perched on a high shelf in her mind, though, waiting until she was ready to use it. Portia was a siren.

★

WHEN CASS WAS GETTING MARRIED, Opal sat by Loch Ness.

The wedding was back at the old house, and Opal had made an appearance, smiled during the toasts, and stayed for a few photographs. She was settled by the glassy frozen lake in her fitted tuxedo, her long hair falling to brush against the stones by the water's edge.

"Winter weddings are harder to sneak away from."

Opal did not turn to Portia. It had been years since their first meeting in Edinburgh, and while she and Opal had grown closer, the latter's family had become even more detached from her. They were an "us," and she was a "her." As the years had unfolded, Opal had found that she could see Portia more clearly.

It didn't change how she felt; it merely framed everything differently. It was completely possible to love someone while knowing that almost every inch of them was just no good at all.

Opal was not in the business of trying to change people. No magic in the world was strong enough to do that.

"I've brought you a plate from the buffet," Portia said, falling down next to Opal in a childlike manner and offering her a plate of salmon and salad. Opal shook her head softly. Portia's hand hovered in the air, still holding the food out like a present.

"What's wrong?" she finally asked quietly.

"Nothing," Opal replied. "I hear you're moving to London. Same as Cass."

"Yes," Portia said. "More my sort of town, I think. Scottish people are so obstinate."

"And hard to manipulate."

"Careful, Opal. Someone might think you actually care."

"I care about my family."

"So do I."

"No. You only care to use them in order to get into the rooms you want to influence."

"I can get into any damn room I want with one word," snapped Portia. Opal closed her eyes. There it was. They were talking about it, facing it. Portia's unspeakably dangerous power, her frightening gift of influence. "I don't need your family to do it."

"Then leave," Opal said, finally looking at her friend.

"Did it ever occur to you that when I saw your magic that day, it made me feel less alone? That it made me feel like there was someone else with this huge power inside them, someone else who knew how it felt?"

"It didn't occur to me," Opal said flatly, "because you don't want anyone else to have any sort of power, Portia."

"You want to talk about power, Opal? You don't use yours."

Opal leaped to her feet and ran at the lake. She heard Portia swear in surprise, but she kept running. As her feet began to slip and skid upon the ice, she vaulted.

And soared.

While her parents possessed no real magic, they had supported the girls. But it was always to be a secret. Perhaps it was Scotland's history that made them cautious. Whatever the reason, magic was a family matter and kept very private.

Opal did not care if anyone saw her fly. She needed it. She needed to leave the world behind and below, be above it all.

When she landed, Portia was staring in amazement. "You're wasting your gifts," Portia finally said softly. "And I can't watch it anymore."

"I don't like what you did to that tourist all those years ago, Sha," Opal replied. "Years of fun and friendship don't wipe it away. I think about it all the time."

"You'll want me around when they turn on you for being different," Portia said calmly, moving to leave. "Believe me."

The witch watched the siren leave, and they would not meet again for years.

CHAPTER TWENTY-THREE

LIKE A CURSE

It all begins to map together for me.

Opal has been conserving her strength and locking herself away in Grandpa's study because of Portia. She has been preparing a spell for Portia. She has not been punishing us or burying her head in the sand, none of the things I secretly thought. She was telling the truth. She had a plan.

It was never about me. It was never meant to be my mission.

I watch Opal take a deep breath before the plunge.

She opens her palms and closes her eyes, her face contorted in effort. It's more exertion than I have ever seen her use. Portia starts to back away, eyeing my aunt with trepidation. "What are you doing?"

"It's a curse," I whisper.

"You can still surrender," Opal gasps, containing the spell between her hands. It's emerald green, and it spits and flares, ready to be unleashed. Portia stares at it.

She swallows and eyes the exit. "Never," she finally says.

My aunt's face saddens, but all she says is "Then this is how it has to be."

Opal releases the curse. It hits the siren with the power of a small explosion, knocking her fully to the floor. I cling to the tree and stare, breathing hard. Opal wipes at her eyes, looking concerned and also crushed. Portia eventually sits up, running her hands over herself as if she's searching for a wound or cut.

"What have you done?" she finally demands.

"You will not die," Opal says softly. "Not because of this. You will not wither away. You're not even injured. But I have cursed you, Sha. I have made you unbelievable."

I hear an intake of breath from Freddy, and Portia frowns, not understanding.

"You have your voice. You have your life. But you will never be believed," Opal goes on. She sounds so mournful. A tear slips free, and I watch it drop. "You will give orders, no one will heed them. You will ask for help, no one will believe you need it. Your power, the gift you misused, it's gone."

Portia's face breaks into an expression of understanding, and then horror dawns. She stares frantically from Opal to me and then to my grandmother.

"Come here, old woman," she barks.

Gran shakes her head. "No."

The siren's frenzied attention moves across every human in the room who, until now, would've succumbed to her spell. They all stand firm, unmoved by her commands. She screams orders at them until her voice cracks, but to no avail.

"Freddy," she finally gasps. "My son, my boy. I love you. You know that, don't you? This was all for you!"

Freddy wipes a tear of his own away. "I didn't believe that before, let alone now."

I can see the exact moment in which Portia realizes that all her power is gone. She lets out a breath and then a silent sob, her forehead dropping to the ground. I look to Opal, expecting to see relief or triumph. No.

My aunt's jaw is shaking as she tries to withhold a sob. Portia's hands grab wretchedly at her, and she allows it, desperately scanning the siren's face for signs of remorse.

"Don't do this to me," Portia says, her words broken apart. "Please, Opal. Don't, anything but this. Kill me! Kill me instead!"

Opal looks up to the ceiling, and I can see that her face is wet with tears. "I forgive you, Sha. Okay? I release you."

Portia is sobbing quietly, Opal's words making her physically recoil. I watch Aunt Leanna put an arm around both Freddy and Marley, slowly starting to lead them away. Freddy watches until he can no longer see Portia. Mum stands guard, her stance prepared for trouble. Gran moves to me, and she is hugging me, trying to extract me from the tree.

"No," I object, clinging on. "No, Gran."

I am not leaving Alona here by herself. If she's still in there somewhere, I don't want her to be trapped in this dark underground kingdom alone.

"Remember the lake in the winter?" Portia breathes, her gaze distant.

Opal smiles sadly. Then, "Yes."

It is another secret between them.

"I wish we were there now," Portia finally utters, before closing her eyes and withdrawing completely.

Opal stands slowly and moves to me. She physically bundles me up so that I'm on my feet, and she helps me walk, guiding me out of the hall. Mum ushers the Ripple out as well, keeping a watchful eye over it as it moves away from Portia and the tree.

"Alona!" I cry, looking back at the silent oak. "It's Alona, I can't leave her."

The adults aren't listening to me now, though. They lead me out of the deep, hidden world and up the winding, narrow stairs to the outside. I can hear Portia crying, her sobs fading the higher we go. Aunt Opal is trembling.

"What will happen to her?" I ask as we near the top and the siren's sounds become almost inaudible.

"I don't know," Opal says. "But at some point, you have to stop listening to the wicked and just leave them to their own misery."

We crawl out of a small entrance carved into the rock. Gran complains the entire time, making me smile. Mum is gently inspecting the Ripple, and Aunt Leanna is gripping both Freddy and Marley in a hug. I relish the cold Scottish wind against my cheeks as I stagger onto the great Arthur's Seat and gaze out at the city.

Aunt Opal stretches her neck, and we all hear it click.

"Oof," she mutters, wincing. She meets my eye. "Not bad for a dead girl, though."

I burst into tears. She's holding me within seconds, and I can tell she is still emotional too. I cling to her, unable to process the fact that she is real.

"I saw it happen," I finally say. "How—"

"Let's all get somewhere warm and dry before we unpack everything," Gran says firmly.

"It's turned midnight," Marley says softly. "It's Christmas Day."

We all huddle together, beside the door to a hidden fortress and beneath the gaze of a great blue dragon, and it's definitely already the hardest, weirdest, best Christmas I have ever had.

CHAPTER TWENTY-FOUR

LUNCH

We go back to my old house, in Stockbridge. Mum makes up the spare room for Freddy and Marley before physically forcing me into my own bed and making me go to sleep. She hugs me for two whole minutes before I drift off, and neither of us says a word. She promises that Dad is in London and totally fine, and that Blue is in the Forth, having fun and chasing the kelpies.

When I wake up, it's almost noon. I can hear movement downstairs, but when I reach the hall, everyone moves out into the garden. Freddy gives me a nod, and Marley and I bump fists, but in the end, only Opal and I are left alone in the dining room.

I sit across from her, and I stare at the improvised

Christmas lunch on the table. Wrapped sweets and croissants.

"What happened?" I finally ask.

She unravels the satin teal pocket square that has been tied around her wrist and lays it on the dining table. "I called in a favor."

"The Stranger?"

"Yes."

I stare at the small scrap of fabric. I remember him giving it to her. "I didn't know he had that power."

"That is . . . all his power is."

"And you knew Portia?"

"In another life, it feels like, but yes. When we were younger."

"You were friends?"

"Yes."

"Like Freddy and me?"

"Sort of."

I try to make sense of this revelation. "Why didn't you tell me?"

She arches an eyebrow in that superior way of hers. "Why didn't you tell me about that dragon? Or your secret trips here?"

I flush, and she nods. "Oh, yes. Marley caved and told us."

I pull a croissant toward me. "Sorry. I've been . . . a version of me I didn't really like."

She smiles gently. "I know that feeling."

"You let Portia live."

"Yes, I did."

"Why?"

"Sometimes you have to ask yourself: Who are you willing to live with and who can't you live without?"

I'm not sure I completely understand, but I nod.

I decide to apologize, feeling all the rash decisions I've made over the last few days now sitting in my stomach. "I'm sorry I wasn't more honest. I'm sorry I didn't listen. I thought because my magic was getting stronger, that meant I could make all the decisions."

She watches me for a moment and then grabs a croissant for herself. "You know?" she says, taking a bite. "There's no one in this world I love more than you. But you drive me absolutely out of my mind."

I snort and burst out a laugh. I glance down at my hands and conjure up the tiniest little flame. "I don't know. I really wanted to be good at something without having to practice."

Opal leans forward. "You're already good enough. Okay? The practice is for you, no one else. You're not in competition with anyone but yourself. You're already great. I just know you can be greater. But that never means you're not enough. You are. You could give up magic tomorrow. It would not lessen you in any of our eyes. Nothing could do that."

I take her words in. I let them cool some of the burns I've been carrying around in me for the last few weeks.

"Who were all those women with Mum and Gran?"

"Other witches. Your mum and grandmother have been gathering allies. Like I said, we had a plan. But thanks to you being kidnapped, we had to bump it forward a bit."

I flush again. "I said sorry."

I don't show how truly embarrassed I am. I thought I had to be the hero. I thought that was my purpose.

"Uh-huh. But don't worry. I should have been honest too. Truth is, that siren and I had a ton of unfinished business, and I didn't want anyone else to handle it but me. Yes, we had a plan, but we should have shared it with you and Marley. I just . . . couldn't come to grips with the idea that we might be recruiting you. Ruining your childhood."

"We wanted to help."

"I know. But the two of you have one job, and that is to be kids. Nothing more. It's not the job of children to fix messes that grown-ups make."

"Full offense, Aunt Opal, but adults seem to make a lot of mess."

"Well." She shrugs. "Amen."

I listen, for a moment, to the happy chatter coming from outside. I can hear Mum laughing and Gran singing "Carol of the Bells." She's doing her funny soprano voice, and I hear Freddy, Marley, and Leanna laughing as well.

"I think everything is going to get a lot better," I finally say.

I stare down at a pile of books by the door. Some of my school worksheets are sitting on the top. Most of them were assigned to me because of my learning difficulty. "Oh," I say, laughing a little hysterically as I lift up the handwriting tasks I've been given. "I was supposed to do these while I was at Loch Ness."

Opal eyes the homework and laughs dryly. "Come on now, Ramya. I don't care if you've been trying to save Scotland, you have to do your pointless anti-neurodiversity exercises."

Suddenly, it's just too funny. The silliness of it.

My school's obsession with trying to fit me into their narrow lines. When I've been flying a dragon and fighting sirens.

There is a knock at the door, and we both look over. The Stranger pokes his head around the frame, and I let out a sound of derision and disbelief.

"How do you keep breaking into our house?" I demand.

"I visit every house eventually," he says calmly.

Opal gets to her feet and hands him the scrap of fabric. "Thanks for the favor."

"You're welcome."

They share a meaningful expression, and then my aunt leaves the room. I stare at the Stranger, and as always when I'm in his presence, I forget the millions of questions I want to ask him. Except one. This time, one remains at the forefront of my mind.

"You said people couldn't come back from the dead."

"I did. But I've been doing this job for a very long time, and exceptions are bound to happen. Timings sometimes are not quite right. Hence why people sometimes live out their doctors' expectations or wake up at the morgue. It happens. Sometimes."

"You said a few days ago, when we were discussing the Ripple, that no spell could bring a human back from death."

"I did. But I did not use a spell on your aunt. I merely . . . looked the other way."

I stare at him in wonder. It never seems possible to say the true reality of who and what he is out loud. He once told me that he had many names. I think I can guess at some of them.

"Yes, spells cannot bring *humans* back from the dead," he confirms cheerfully. "Now"—he scoops up a sweet, unwraps it, and pops it into his mouth—"nonhumans, on the other hand. That's a different tale. They could be brought back if their hex were reversed. It would take quite the witch to do it, though."

I suddenly understand his meaning, and my eyes widen in shock and desperate hope. He smiles and tips his hat.

"Merry Christmas, Ramya. Eat lots and sleep well. You've earned it." Then he is gone.

★

I FIND MARLEY IN THE FRONT ROOM, by the fire. I slowly sit down beside him.

"It's strange, isn't it?" he eventually says. "Living through something?"

That is exactly what this has felt like, I realize. As if our story is no longer our own, and we've been part of something massive and shattering. Something that will change the way we see things from now on.

We're not the same as we were last Christmas.

"It's always going to be you and me," I tell him quietly. "I'm sorry my thinking got so black and white. I'm sorry I kept believing I was the chosen one."

He laughs at that. "You're the one with all the magic. I thought you were the chosen one too."

"Turns out Aunt Opal was, and we're just pawns."

He shrugs. "I don't think of it like that."

I frown. "No?"

"No. That's how Portia would think. Ren, too. That's how they view everything. So we shouldn't think like that. You're important. I'm important. And we tried to do the right thing."

He says it so simply. Turning the complexities of this weird adventure into the most elegant terms.

"You're the best person I know," I tell him.

He looks at me and smiles. "Even if my brain gets a bit weird too? A bit panicky?"

I'm surprised to hear him voice it. I know he gets anxious. I can see it, and I never know how to help him. "Yes. Because of that."

I'm often too stupid to be scared. Marley is smart enough to know the cost of everything, and he makes himself be brave anyway. That makes him the most courageous person I know.

We don't need to say anything else, so we shuffle into the kitchen. Everyone is gathered around the small table, and Mum is using her craft to light candles.

Freddy sings for us. His voice is astounding, the true gift of a siren. He doesn't order or compel a single person to do his bidding, he just shares the magnificence of his voice. Everyone is calmer. Everyone can breathe.

He sings "In the Bleak Midwinter" for us all, and I finally feel at peace.

EPILOGUE

EDINBURGH IN MARCH

"There he is, I can see him coming out."

Mum, Opal, Leanna, Marley, and I are all waiting outside Freddy's fancy school in Edinburgh. Marley and I have just been picked up from our own, and now we're meeting my siren friend. He lives with Leanna and Marley these days, and even my cousin has to admit that he's starting to like the siren.

Freddy saunters over, and the adults move away, giving us some privacy. It's been months since Portia's demise, and I know they worry about Freddy. Not about his influence, but about how he is coping. Some days are great for him, and others are not.

Marley and I try to be good enough friends to him that we can take some of that burden away.

"Lord, your school is posh," I mutter, looking him up and down.

He laughs. "Thanks. I'm surprised they let the likes of you near the gate."

"I'll put a stop to places like this when I run the world, never you fear."

He laughs again and then glances down at his shoes. "So listen. At this rather posh school, they want us to, like, socialize and stuff. There's a spring ball thing they're throwing, and we're allowed to bring a friend. I was wondering, if you weren't busy a week from Friday, if you wanted to come?"

Marley stifles a snort and turns away. I glare at my cousin and then find that I am now staring at my own shoes. "With you?"

"Well, yeah."

"As a date?"

"Yeah."

I glance over and see a group of girls staring at us.

One gives me a slow perusal, but another smiles encouragingly. It all seems too normal and friendly and like what we're supposed to be doing.

I suppose it's funny that getting asked to a dance is scarier to me right now than dragons, kelpies, and vampires.

"You wouldn't rather go with one of them?" I ask, nodding toward the girls.

He follows my glance. "Nah. They'd probably be nice to me. Where's the fun in that?"

"Ramya? Rams!"

I close my eyes in mortification at the sound of Mum and my two aunts hollering at us from ten feet away.

"Put the boy out of his misery!" Opal calls, while her sisters cackle like the witches they are.

"We can go dress shopping, or you can wear one of mine!" Mum adds.

"Oh, vintage," Leanna pipes up.

They all guffaw, and I can feel myself turning crimson. I grab Freddy by the elbow and move him as far away from my humiliating family as I can.

"This isn't a joke?" I mutter.

"Of course not."

"If it is, I'll kill you."

"It's not."

I scuff my shoe and shrug. "Okay, then. Fine. I'll go with you. But if the music sucks, I'm leaving. Dyspraxics can dance, but only if the music is decent."

I am so embarrassed, I can't look at him for long. I do notice that he's beaming, but I turn and rush back toward Marley. I have something else I need to do this week, and now is the perfect time, because I can't take the teasing I know my family will deliver. Marley walks in step beside me as I storm away.

"Do not say a single word to me," I snap at him. I can feel the mirth radiating off him.

" 'Sirens are evil, Marley,' " he says, spluttering with laughter and pitching his voice high as he does a terrible impersonation of me. " 'We've got to stop them. We've got to make sure—' "

"Shut. Up."

" 'Just not my boyfriend, he's different.' "

"I will end you. I will pound you into these cobblestones and Edinburgh ghost guides will point at you and make tourists give them money. Here lies Marley, cousin of Ramya Knox. He died of not minding his own business."

"I'll book the church hall for you both!" Opal yells, making Marley shriek.

"I hate you all!" I call back.

★

BLUE NUZZLES AGAINST MY HAND as Marley and I reach the hillside of Arthur's Seat.

"You're getting too brazen, girl," I tell her. "Anyone could see you."

She chuffs and I laugh. We are far up, tucked in near the entrance to the old kingdom. Finding the door took a bit of searching, but we located it eventually.

I've been practicing. Every single day after school, I read books and practice with Aunt Opal.

Preparing for this moment.

I cast a shield, one that has Glamour built in. We will not be disturbed by hillwalkers or geology classes on this day. I open the door hidden in the great rock and ask Blue to stand guard as Marley and I step inside the darkness and begin our descent. I cast a little flame, and we use it to light our way.

"What if Portia is here?" Marley whispers nervously.

I'm concentrating on the steps but then decide to let magic take over. I float, my feet airborne above the stone, and I glide down toward the lower ground. I land gracefully.

As I said, I've been practicing.

I wait for Marley, and we push open the great wooden doors together. We hold our breath, both secretly and silently worrying that the siren might still be here.

She is not. Only the tree stands, solitary and unmoving, in the center of the ample hall.

I walk slowly toward the oak.

I've been practicing. Every day. When I'm not, I think about it. I think about improvement when I go to sleep, and I wake up with the answers. I remember what the Stranger said, even if his face is blurry.

It would take quite the witch to do it.

I am the witch to do it.

I begin to conjure. The spell is pinkish and light, buzzing between my hands with electric energy and a need to be cast. It is strong, stronger than anything I have ever done, but I am calm as I prepare to release it.

I am not defined by handwriting workshops. Or the disapproval of others. I am not even defined by my family. This feeling, this ability, these hands that are able to create despite the strain they are sometimes under, that is what I choose to be defined by. In moments like this, I have learned to let the blue inside me go.

When magic is blue, it's not for you. I was told that once.

I let all colors of magic inside my heart. The darker tones, the lighter shades, the fire and the water and the earth.

The pink turns into a pale blue, and I know that I am ready. I cast. I release. The spell breaks loose and hits the trunk of the tree with the force of an arrow shooting through the air.

A branch begins to slowly transform, bark becoming flesh. Nimble twigs snap into bone, fingers that are reaching out for someone. The roots become two legs, bent into a crouching position. The withered leaves meld together and become hair.

A still and unmoving tree transforms into a dryad

before our eyes. She stays crouched, her head hung low for a few seconds, before she breathes in a huge gulp of air and looks up.

We stare at each other.

Then, as her chapped lips part to say my name, I throw my arms around her and squeeze. I hold on with as much strength as I used all those months ago, when I thought I would never see her again.

It's a spell I could've only cast in my dreams last year, but I made it happen. I hold on, too emotional to let go.

Her hand touches my face, as if she can't believe I am real. Then it travels up to my head, feeling the woolen garment I am now wearing with pride.

I put it away, with some parts of myself, and I want to wear them all again. No more masks, no more hidden places. I know that sometimes I might misplace pieces of myself. I might forget a part of myself in a rude conversation or a bad deed. Someone might pass on and take pieces of me with them. Maybe some pieces are gone, and they won't come back.

Maybe that's fine. Maybe you grow new parts of yourself, or other pieces get stronger. I've been made to feel incomplete my whole life, but that is not the story at all.

"Nice hat," Alona says.

"It's, uh, not a hat," I say, stroking it fondly. "It's a beret."

"You came back for me," she whispers, her voice a croak after being unused for so long.

"I told you. Friends always come back."

Wherever the pieces of me go, I know who I am. I know that the fragments that need to return will always find a way back, and that what is most important will never truly be gone.

I'll be fine.

The End.

ACKNOWLEDGMENTS

Thank you to the NHS and its incredible staff for taking care of me during the writing and editing of this novel.

Thank you to Josh. We have now survived moving house, and I finally have an office. I can't wait to write a new book in it.

Thank you to Lauren, Justine, Paul, and the hard-working staff at BLM Agency.

Thank you to everyone involved in the adaptation of *A Kind of Spark:* 9Story, the crew, the writers, and the incredible actors. It hasn't aired while I'm writing this, but your work has been astounding.

Thank you to the whole team at Knights Of for never boxing me in. Congrats on the most deserved Nibbie of all time!

Thank you to Annabelle at EDPR. You are the

John Williams to my movie. As in, without you, I'm pretty unimpressive.

Thank you to Frank Cottrell-Boyce for being an example of kindness, community, and all that's important in this funny little job.

Thank you to Jennifer Bell for fun on the South Bank.

Thank you to Faridah for late-night Instagram chats.

Thank you to Maisie Chan, Benjamin Dean, Aisha Bushby, and Ross Montgomery for a brilliant Edinburgh International Book Festival. I pray it's not my last.

To Maz Evans, Piers Torday, M. G. Leonard, and Sam Sedgman for a healing night in the pub before my debut at the Hay Festival. Thank you to Maya for telling me where to go and what to do when I was completely alone.

Thank you to the readers. You're always better than I remember, and my memories are very fond and warm.

Thank you to my family.

Thank you to Eishar for spontaneously agreeing to a sequel and for always being the best in the business.

Thank you to Bounce and to so many incredible bookshops.

Thank you to Books Are My Bag, Waterstones, the Little Rebels Award, Blackwell's, and BookTrust.

Thank you to all the incredible schools who have read my books and invited me for a visit. You're all wonderful, as are your students.

Thank you to Kay Wilson for her consistent excellence.

Thank you to every single person who generously offered to help with the Adrien Prize.

Addie, Cora, and Ramya changed my life. Thank you if you've let them into yours. I mean it. I've thought about giving up on this painful, frightening, exposing, and often classist job. A job where I always feel like the poorest, weakest, and most uneducated person in the room.

People who actually like your stories are the only balm. So thank you. I'll hold on for as long as I can.

Thank you to the booksellers. Without them, this industry would merely be a race to the bottom.

ABOUT THE AUTHOR

Elle McNicoll is a bestselling and award-winning novelist. Her debut, *A Kind of Spark,* was a Blue Peter Book Awards Best Story winner, an overall winner of the Waterstones Children's Book Prize, and a Blackwell's Book of the Year. She has been nominated for the Carnegie Medal and was shortlisted for the Books Are My Bag Readers Awards, the Branford Boase Award, and the Little Rebels Children's Book Award. Her second novel, *Show Us Who You Are,* was a Blackwell's Books of the Month title and one of the *Bookseller*'s Best Books of the year. She is an advocate for better representation of neurodiversity in publishing and currently lives in West London.

ellemcnicoll.com

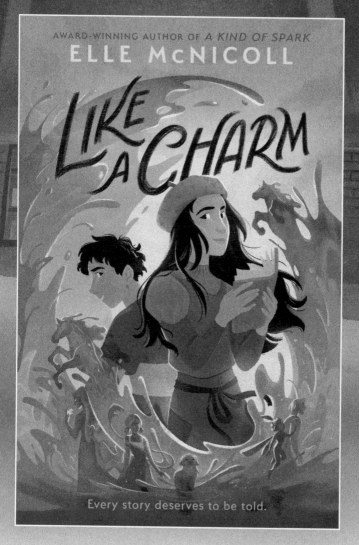

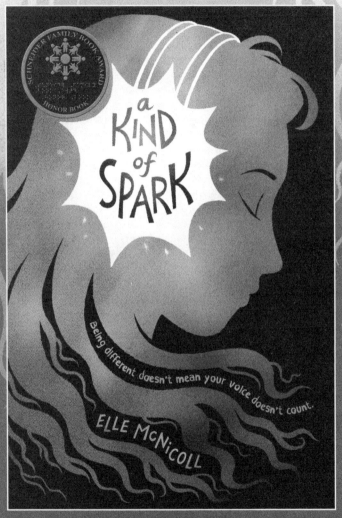